HERSHELE

A Jewish Love Story

HERSHELE
A Jewish Love Story

Jacob Dinezon

Translated from the Yiddish by
Jane Peppler

Edited and with an Introduction by
Scott Hilton Davis

Published by
Jewish Storyteller Press
2016

Cover painting by Amy F. Levine

Translated from
Hershele: roman
Yakov Dinezon
Published by Ahisefer, Warsaw, Poland
Copyright 1928 by S. Sreberk, New York, U.S.A.

Published by
Jewish Storyteller Press
Raleigh, North Carolina, U.S.A.
www.jewishstorytellerpress.com
books@jewishstorytellerpress.com

Printed in the United States

Learn more about Jacob Dinezon at www.jacobdinezon.com

ISBN 978-0-9798156-7-6

Library of Congress Control Number: 2015958692

For Robin and Jim Evans

Introduction

Jacob Dinezon was a successful and beloved 19th century Jewish writer who played a central role in the development of Yiddish as a literary language. A contemporary and mentor to Sholem Aleichem, author of the Tevye stories, Dinezon's small apartment in Warsaw, Poland became a meeting place for both established and aspiring Jewish writers. His professional partnership with the Yiddish author I. L. Peretz blossomed into a life-long friendship.

Dinezon achieved fame as a Jewish author in 1877 with the publication of his first novel, *The Dark Young Man*. A sentimental and romantic potboiler, the book elicited copious tears from its readers and quickly sold out its first printing of 10,000 copies. Considered Yiddish literature's first bestseller, *The Dark Young Man* established Dinezon as the "Father of the Jewish realistic romance."

Hershele: A Jewish Love Story first appeared in 1891 as part of a literary journal Dinezon published in partnership with Peretz. Dinezon's story is about a young yeshiva boy whose love for the daughter of a rich widow is complicated by his growing interest in the modern ideas of the Jewish Enlightenment and those in the religious community trying to block his path. Woven into the story are many of the conflicts facing Eastern European Jewry at the end of the 19th century: shtetl politics, cruel treatment of the poor by the wealthy, the harsh conditions endured by Talmud scholars living in study houses, the hopeful draw of the Enlightenment and modern ideas, the changing views about romantic love, and the consequences of arranged marriages. The story's final outcome, as in all of Dinezon's novels, is heart-rending and thought-provoking.

Although Jacob Dinezon continued to write into the first decade of the 20th century, he spent the final years of his life as a social reformer and philanthropist, working to advance secular Jewish education and caring for children orphaned during the First World War. When he died in 1919, Jews in the tens of thousands came out onto the streets of Warsaw to mourn their beloved Yiddish writer.

ONE

He spent his days and nights learning in the yeshiva, the study house, and received a charity meal from her mother once a week. If that day fell on Chanukah, the New Moon at the beginning of the month, or on some mid-week holiday, he might also taste a bit of meat. But on most ordinary Wednesdays, he ate little more than what was provided in the donated meal.

Her mother was Brayndl, a rich widow, very stingy by nature. Although everyone knew she was stingy, she didn't know they knew—and would have preferred they didn't. There were, God be praised, already enough angry mouths with nothing better to do than gossip about her. She never willingly chose to pledge towards a charity or good deed; and when she couldn't find some simple excuse to avoid a contribution, it always cost her considerable heartache—not to mention a few coins.

"One mustn't be a scoundrel," she consoled herself. "One can't scrimp before the living God. He knows I'm a desolate widow and that my little bit of money is my whole livelihood. People, on the other hand, seem to think I have sacks of gold. When there's no alternative I give, though I really can't afford it."

9

Which is why she agreed, for the sake of a relative who was the head of the yeshiva where she prayed, to take on the responsibility of providing one meal a week to a poor student. She thought to herself, "Sad to say, if I'm not careful, the boy will eat me out of house and home. So I'll let him just get by with leftovers." But when the first boy arrived, she soon realized that bread was also slipping down his throat.

"*Vey iz mir,*" she exclaimed to herself. "He eats in such an unnatural fashion. I've never seen a lovely scholar eating like such a peasant. A fellow like this could eat up everything in my pantry!" So first thing the next morning, she asked her relative, the head of the yeshiva, to send her a different boy.

"Why doesn't he please you?" he asked her.

"He somehow seems unhealthy," she replied smoothly. "You know my Mirele is a very delicate child. I'm afraid, God forbid, she'll catch a sickness from this poor boy."

"Sickness? Him? I wish his robust health for all my own children!" said the head of the yeshiva.

"But I tell you, he doesn't eat like a healthy boy," declared Brayndl. "Have you ever seen such a thing in your life: a fellow eating with both his fists? It must be some defect in him, God forbid. I hope he doesn't die from it! I ask you: send me a quiet boy, a refined child, one you can sit at the table with."

But on the following Wednesday, when a different student came to eat with her, she found this boy had the same sickness—he ate when he was hungry. She exchanged the second boy for a third, and the third boy for a fourth. No student ever ate at her home for a whole semester.

She felt envious watching her neighbor's schoolboy eat. "You have such an elegant, refined child at your table; one can see by the way he eats that he's a fine scholar. I have no luck with the boys

I'm sent—big, overgrown ones that only know how to eat. They don't say a word about the Gemara. I don't even know if I get credit for a mitzvah if all my boy does is eat!"

Everyone soon knew about Brayndl's miserly nature and the sort of meal to expect from her. Quiet schoolboys, often waiting an hour or two before she remembered them, preferred to go hungry rather than be humiliated at her table. If someone could, in fact, be found to eat a charity meal at her house on a Wednesday, he'd most likely be one of the bolder boys who wanted to tear into her bread as a way of avenging his embarrassed brethren, those with whom she'd found fault in order to be rid of them.

Thus, both sides carried on a war—the heroes of the yeshiva showing their eating prowess, and Brayndl plotting to make their bitter bread even more bitter. She constantly came up with excuses to get away with poorly prepared meals. Sometimes there was no container of water needed for the ritual hand washing before eating. Sometimes the food simply ran out at the exact moment before the meal—and with the serving maid away at the marketplace, so there was no one to send for a fresh loaf of bread. "You'll just have to make do with the little bit that's here!" Brayndl would say apologetically.

Very often some excuse would be made. She poured out stories of aggravation on the poor hungry yeshiva student about the obstacles she encountered preparing the mid-day meal, or how it had somehow become unkosher, or other long explanations why she no longer had a morsel of food to put in his mouth.

Another time she told the maid to give the poor boy something to eat, then locked up everything in the pantry and prepared to go out. "What have I got to give him, dear mistress?" the maid asked.

"Give him whatever you've got."

"And for a second course?"

"Whatever, just something," she answered as she slammed the door behind her.

In the yeshiva, her two courses received names. The first was called, "Whatever you've got," and the second, "Whatever, just something." On the day it was Brayndl's turn to feed him, a boy had two choices: he'd have to be given some money, or he'd have to put up with hunger and shame in order to take vengeance on the shrew.

Finally, God saw her misery and sent her a boy of the exact sort she wanted: a quiet child, not much of an eater, but one who was so refined and shy that she often came to him and asked him to eat a bit more. This boy was Hershele.

Because the head of the yeshiva needed a favor from Brayndl, he convinced Hershele to accept her paltry Wednesday meal. He then arranged for Hershele—who certainly deserved it for his clever head, zeal, and quietness—to take his Thursday meal with Borekh the butcher. Borekh was known to provide the best charity meal in the whole village.

But over time, Hershele came to enjoy Brayndl's Wednesdays more than Borekh's Thursdays. Her house was always clean, rich, and bright—it was a pleasure to sit there even without anything to eat. Borekh's house was always dirty and full of shouting and tumult. And though Hershele quickly became tired of eating, Borekh's wife hurled more of everything onto his plate. He could barely finish one piece of meat before she laid on another. He sweated, lost his strength to eat, and tried to slow down to catch his breath, but Borekh shouted in his butcher's voice: "As long as you have a soul in you, keep at it! If you eat as you should, you'll also learn as you should. Eat like a big fellow and that will give you the strength to be a big fellow before the Torah, which I know can sap your strength!"

While eating at Brayndl's, Hershele felt more refined, but at Borekh's he became coarser, stuffing himself with meat, *kishke,* and tripe, and listening to coarse words, curses, and abuse—words he was embarrassed to even think about.

Borekh found only one defect in his yeshiva student: "If only he had the strength to eat as he should. He's a great boy. He can explain the law or a complicated story from the holy Torah. If he'd just eat like a proper person!"

Brayndl, on the other hand, found this a fine trait in Hershele. "He's a refined child, very genteel," she'd say, "quiet as a mouse, eats like a bird. No matter how much one gives him, he thinks it's too much. God grant that he'll eat up what I don't begrudge giving him—I know I'm getting a mitzvah through this."

The head of the yeshiva praised him, too. "It's a pleasure to teach such a student," he'd say each time Hershele asked questions concerning the Gemara, then answered them himself according to what the great rabbis would say. "He has such fine sensibilities; he's becoming a real individual!"

Hershele considered the head of the yeshiva almost as dear to him as a father. He also loved his friends, though it seldom happened in the study house that one schoolboy loved another. In addition to his kindness to them—he sometimes slipped them a solution in class or found them some clever thought about the Gemara—and his quiet humility, Hershele had yet another charm in their eyes: his beautiful singing voice. He often sang lovely tunes while studying the Gemara, or simply broke into a happy song without knowing why. Overhearing him, his friends declared, "Miracle of miracles. A gift from God!"

On long winter nights they'd gather around and ask him to sing a lively folk-tune, a cantor's melody, or a fantasia. He sang everything from Christian songs and choral pieces, to melodies from the Purim play, "The Selling of Joseph," and biblical plays such as "Saul's Kingdom" and "The Greatness of David and Solomon."

Every yeshiva boy learned a special tune from him, and it made studying the Gemara easier and sweeter. The tunes blew soul into the words and filled the study house with gusto, pleasure, and Torah. Even lazy boys became diligent.

Hershele, too, always studied with a tune, but it varied. Often one could hear in the melody his happiness and pleasure as he studied the teaching within the Gemara. Sometimes one heard a deep sadness, an unfamiliar hopefulness, or a kind of longing, as though his soul was trying to tear itself out and fly somewhere high above to be with those whose wise words he now studied.

This winter, however, his tunes changed. Every day they became deeper, sadder, more moving. One could hear in them a hidden heartache, and it was hard for the listener to bear. One wanted to console him, fall on his neck, kiss, and embrace him.

His eyes glistened, his always-wet cheeks burned, and as the tune grew deeper, the words of the Gemara poured out like pearls. He was studying so intently, he didn't see that a friend, standing nearby to listen, had tears in his eyes, too. He studied and sang ever more deeply as his tears poured out. Finally the friend asked, "Tell me, Hershele, what's the matter? Why do you lament so? Your tune would shatter a stone!"

Suddenly Hershele awoke as if from a dream. A heavy sigh escaped his lips as he closed the Gemara and began pacing back and forth in the study house as if seeking something he lacked.

His friends had often debated his heavenly voice, yet they all agreed that beyond the miraculous sound itself, Hershele expressed such great feeling that if he only learned to read music, he could give concerts for princes and lords just as the operatic cantor of Vilna, the "Vilner Balebesl," had done in his day. But

Hershele had no interest in concerts. He never desired to sing what others asked for. He sang because it was his nature. He sang what was in his heart, and he didn't even know why. Torah and the Gemara, they were the point; anyone, it seemed to him, could sing.

"It's not the throat," he told everyone, "it's the heart that sings. If another had as full a heart, he'd sing the same way." And it bothered him to hear his friends make so much of him and praise his voice right to his face.

Yet, he really wanted *her* to hear him sing—to come into the study house while he sat under the Holy Ark studying the Gemara. He wouldn't see her—nobody would see her—but she would hear all his melodies and the embellishments which flowed from him so sweetly.

He knew that she sang, too, that she loved singing, but he was angry at himself for wanting such a thing, something which could never be. "Fool!" he told himself. "Why do you want this? And what would happen if she did hear you? How could I even talk to her? What could I even talk to her about? She's refined, a rich man's only daughter, what business does she have with me? And she carries herself so proudly."

Still, he wanted—just once in his life—to sing out to her fully and completely. Perhaps things would be easier for him then. His heart would be peaceful and pure, and he would sing happily again without sadness.

The more he thought about this, the more she stood before his eyes. He began to feel her presence drawing him towards her. He couldn't forget her. He even thought about her while studying, and could no longer hear himself reciting the words.

He asked himself, "Is this not the *yetzer hore,* the Evil Inclination, standing before me? Is it some kind of enchantment? She's never exchanged a word with me, barely glanced at me, and yet I can't forget her eyes! When I think of her, my heart feels empty, torn out. It's true sorcery!"

He began to seek talismans and passages from holy books with advice about all the sicknesses in the world. He also began studying with greater diligence, probing more deeply into the matter, praying piously not to hear the Evil Inclination which he knew would carry him to no good end.

Of all the healing remedies, the only one possible for him was fasting. After all, who didn't know that Hershele cared little for eating? Ever since the Evil Inclination began tormenting him, he'd lost his appetite completely. He fasted mercilessly; only another deeply-felt pain could help him forget his heartache.

The fasting, however, was in vain: the weaker he grew from not eating, the stronger the fantasy grew within him. He saw her clearly, even when he prayed with closed eyes; she prayed, too, and sang in his mind, though his eyes were focused on the prayer book. He could see her and hear her every word, each a pearl from her lovely mouth. With his eyes closed, he could see her and hear her song in pure, clear Hebrew, yet he never realized it was not her voice he heard, but his own.

Suddenly the congregation began to say Kaddish. He had lost his place and didn't know where he was. As he began to recite Kaddish with the others, tears sprang from his eyes for his sinful thoughts while praying, and he asked God to send him a remedy for his ailing soul.

The same thing happened with the Gemara. He couldn't study without a tune, but as soon as he started, a fountain of melody poured out of him. He forgot the world, the Gemara, and it seemed she stood near him, listening, singing with him. His tears began to fall over the Gemara, and they awoke him from his heavy dream. "The Evil Inclination," he sighed. "What does it want from me?"

Two

She was Mirele, Brayndl's only daughter, a lively maiden with beautiful blue eyes and long blond braids, slender and graceful, well brought up, supple; one could see her good heart in her radiant eyes.

Everyone who had known her dead father said she was just like him. He, too, was good and happy. But Brayndl had shortened his years; she wanted him to be a harsh moneylender, but he didn't have it in him. She made him sick and only realized what a crown, what a golden husband she was losing when he was lying on his deathbed.

Before he died, he placed a few thousand rubles into the reliable hands of his brother-in-law, Brayndl's brother, to be saved for Mirele's dowry. All the rest he left to Brayndl with the hope that one day she would have a happier life with a second husband if she remarried after his death. From the interest on the three thousand rubles, she could educate her daughter as the modern world demanded.

After her husband's death, Brayndl decided not to take a new husband. She remained a widow, raising her only daughter, haggling with rabbis and teachers, and building her lending business.

As far as the town teachers could manage it, Mirele was well-educated and refined. She had the finest handwriting, wrote in Russian and Yiddish, and could decipher the most difficult script. Her teacher Nekhemye, a far-seeing and accomplished man, also taught her German, a bit of French, and, as he himself had a good voice, he taught her to sing.

At first, Brayndl objected. "What good is that to me? Will she be a cantor in the women's *shul?*"

Nekhemye said a proper education includes everything, even singing. "One should have skills and not need them, and what harm if she sings, since it's a pleasure for her? Indulge her, she's your only daughter."

A pleasure? Then let it be so. Brayndl agreed, shrugging over the craziness of a girl singing.

Mirele never took part in her mother's business, though she would plead sometimes on behalf of one of the customers. But Brayndl replied, "It's not your affair. Taking pity on others is cruelty to oneself. When you're older, you'll know your mother is not, God forbid, like the barefoot people in the street. I only take what is due me after the business is completed. What matter if a few extra kopecks come my way?"

Yet Brayndl found nothing too expensive for her only daughter. If only she would eat. It would make her so healthy. But the girl, who spoiled her appetite with little snacks, came to the table only for her mother's sake. She was utterly unable to convince Brayndl to be generous with whoever else was there as well.

At first she looked at Hershele the way she looked at all the other boys, though she'd often heard her mother praise him for his quiet gentility. She'd also heard he was a good student and sang like a violin.

Once Brayndl gave Mirele the same spoon Hershele had eaten with an hour earlier. Mirele laid it aside and asked for the keys to the silver chest to take out another. But Brayndl couldn't find the keys and told her to eat with the spoon she'd been given.

"I can't eat with this spoon," Mirele replied.

"What's the matter with it? Is it unclean?"

"The schoolboy just ate with it," Mirele said, not really sure why she was blushing.

"It won't hurt you a bit," her mother answered. "I suspect to his own mother and father he's just as delicate a child as you are. Don't you see what a refined boy he is? Torah shines in his face!"

"He's a schoolboy," said Mirele.

"What's the matter with that? Your father himself, may he rest in peace, studied barefoot at the yeshiva. Do you think all schoolboys are the same? Hershele, our schoolboy, is certainly of the finest pedigree, and it won't do him any harm when it comes to a match that he studied in the yeshiva. I wish I had a stick of gold for the fine bride he will have someday. Don't be ugly about it, my daughter; don't let it bother you."

"But I really can't use this spoon, Mama."

"Don't sin, my child, it's forbidden to say such things! You're killing me. What's the matter? What have you seen in him that makes you so uneasy about his spoon?"

Maybe her mother was right, Mirele thought. Perhaps Hershele was different from all the others. Something about him was quiet and thoughtful; he often looked at her with expression and shyness.

As she sat at the table on the Wednesdays that followed, she studied him closely and saw that he was handsome. Unintentionally, she looked straight into his eyes. They looked back at her and her heart felt a tug. His eyes seemed to say, "Have pity, don't laugh at my poverty." When he left, she was sorry she'd embarrassed him with her glances. She worried he might have thought she mocked him, which was not her intention at all.

Later she heard stories about his singing and praying before the congregation on the first Sabbath of the month. She loved singing. She'd give half her soul for beautiful singing and wanted to talk with him about it. But how? He became very embarrassed when she started a conversation; his look said, "Have pity on me, don't laugh at my poverty."

She didn't ask herself why he was so bashful. She knew a yeshiva boy should be modest, and he was also shy in front of her mother. Even the serving maid asked him why he was so shy. So why shouldn't he be this way with her as well? Perhaps he was embarrassed by his poor clothes; perhaps he had not been born a pauper.

Her heart ached. Why was he so poor? She wanted to know about his parents and where he came from. Did he have a sister, or at least a rich uncle somewhere to whom she could write, saying, "It's time to send some new clothes and not let your dear nephew be so humiliated by his poverty."

She decided to speak to him herself, to ask about his family, to find a chance to explain that a person should not feel beaten down by poverty. To explain, casually, that she would never, God forbid, make fun of him. That on the contrary, she wished him all the best. That she knew he was a good scholar; that she'd heard people praise his beautiful singing voice, which was worth more to her than riches or anything else.

One day, while her mother was away visiting her uncle, Mirele came in from the street. She was flushed and ran through the dining room where Hershele was waiting for Brayndl to call him to wash before his meal. She suddenly realized that this was the time she could eat and talk with him at the table.

Hershele's heart told him she wanted to have a word with him. She'd thrown him a glance as she ran by, as if to say, "It's good you're here. Now I can tell you how offended I am that you're always thinking of me!"

She certainly must've known he thought about her all the time—otherwise she wouldn't have looked at him so often. And she certainly must be angry, and rightly so. "Where do I, a yeshiva boy, get the right to think of her?" He prepared to hear himself shamed and rebuked. But before he could think of a way to save himself, she was back. He dropped his head, his eyes fixed on the floor but not seeing it. It seemed to him he saw only her lovely eyes looking at him with compassion, humanity, and love.

"Who knows?" he thought. "Perhaps she means to say a good word to me. It must be true, what the world says: 'One heart senses another.' But if she asks me, what shall I answer? Nothing. I won't answer her at all. I can't answer; better to be silent. She's clever, she'll sense on her own that silence is an admission." His head dropped lower, but his heart beat more loudly.

"Hershl," he heard a voice behind him say, as lovely as a voice from heaven. "Hershl!" he heard again, and wanted to answer. But first he'd have to breathe out. Why was he so afraid?

"Why don't you answer?" Mirele asked, coming closer. "Will you not even speak one word to me?"

He released his breath with a heavy sigh, but he couldn't speak. Unwillingly, his eyes turned towards her dear, sweet voice. He looked Mirele in the face, but didn't see her. His head grew heavy, leaden; his heart suddenly stopped beating. He saw flaming wheels before his eyes and had to grab the edge of the table so as not to fall from his chair.

Seeing his paleness and trembling limbs, Mirele asked fearfully, "What's the matter with you, Hershele?" Hershele—little Hershl—

the diminutive name her mother always called him. In her terrified state, she forgot it wasn't suitable for her to be so familiar with him, but he didn't notice.

"Hershele, you're not well," she said, bringing him a glass of water. "Here, drink this," she implored him, but as he reached for the glass, his hand trembled and he spilled half the water on the tablecloth.

She raised the glass to his lips and he took a sip. "Thank you. Thank you," he whispered.

"Are you dizzy from the charcoal fumes?" she asked softly.

"No, no, it's nothing. But there, in the study house—" he was barely able to make up a reason.

"Lie down a while here on the sofa, Hershele, until you feel better. Don't be embarrassed." She took him by the hand and led him to the sofa where she arranged a pillow and told him to lie down.

He wanted to go back to the yeshiva, but a moment later, Mirele and the serving maid returned from the kitchen with a bowl of warm water. They told him to put a wet cloth on his head, though it was only his heart that ached—it hurt him terribly to have caused Mirele such fear and worry.

Mirele believed he'd been overcome by fumes and tried to soothe his headache. With her own hands she cut slices of lemon and laid them on his temples. For the first time she saw his handsome forehead and lovely hair—previously always covered by his poor cap. Her heart filled with compassion for him.

She left the room so he could sleep a little. But how could he sleep? He was so ashamed of himself and this farcical comedy he was playing; he had to pretend to sleep and pretend his head still hurt so she wouldn't notice something else had caused his faintness. He didn't know how to give the "something else" a name. But

God knew it wasn't his fault; it was an Evil Inclination, a visitation; he'd been taken against his will. With such painful thoughts, he lay there for an hour, two, three.

"How can one get up and leave?" he asked himself. "I should say I've recovered. Shall I go in to her? Is that suitable? How can I tell her? If she'd come ask how I'm doing, I could tell her—but to go to her all of a sudden, out of the blue, and say, 'Listen, I'm feeling better.' How could I do that? Wouldn't my tongue stick to the roof of my mouth again?"

He asked God to make Mirele come into the room and inquire; he asked God to ensure he'd be able to speak clearly and be respectable in her eyes, so she herself would suggest that he go back to the study house.

Suddenly the door opened and Mirele entered. She walked quietly so as not to wake the patient if he were still sleeping. She looked like a pretty angel, and he felt like a wandering shepherd in one of those sorcerer's stories told in the study house, who finds himself near a princess in a crystal palace.

"Are you feeling better?" she asked with a soft smile.

"Yes, better. I can go home now."

"Surely you don't live at the yeshiva?"

He wasn't sure how to answer the question.

"Do you have a home nearby?" she asked.

"I don't have a home—not a home with parents, I mean. But I can go back to the yeshiva now."

"That's not good; you could take ill again."

He almost said she shouldn't worry about him, but thought better of it. "I'll sleep in the tailors' study house," he said.

"Do you have things there?" she asked.

Again he didn't understand the question and thought maybe she knew he was lying to her. He looked at her, mortified.

His look, however, moved Mirele profoundly. Suddenly she remembered: "You still haven't eaten today. Wait here, I'll get you something to eat!"

"No, I must go," he begged her.

"But you aren't well. Spend the night here."

"No—thank you. Good day. God will repay you for your good heart."

And with these words, Hershele turned towards the door and fled, as if from a fire. He was happy that at least his last few words to Mirele had been clearly stated; that was all he really wanted. Maybe it was all worth it, just for the chance to say them.

When Hershele finally reached the study house—and in order not to be caught in his lie—he laid down in a corner and said he'd almost fainted. One of the older schoolboys who had once taken Wednesday meals at Brayndl's, cursed her and said Hershele had probably gotten faint waiting for the old witch to remember to feed him. This angered Hershele, who replied sharply, "You're sinning, you ingrate. She wasn't even home."

"That's not the point," the schoolboy said, "may the devil take her father and her father's father! How many times did I feel faint at her house? Why are you standing up for her?"

"Because I eat her bread and salt, so I won't listen to you curse her!" And he meant it. To Hershele's surprise, Brayndl had, unbeknownst to her, awakened a defender in him. Not through any virtues of her own, but because she was Mirele's mother. For Mirele's sake, Brayndl was now dear to him.

"You're all ungrateful sinners," Hershele said to his comrades. "One shouldn't even say a word to you!"

A fight might have broken out between the boys, but Hershele suddenly remembered it was wrong to show such anger to his friends. He silenced his adversary with a cry of pain, "Oy!"

The next day, Hershele didn't go for his charity meal, even though it was on a different street, far from Brayndl's house. "It wouldn't do," he told himself, "to seem recovered so quickly. What if Mirele sends someone to check on me? It would look better if I were lying down."

And sure enough, as he suspected, Brayndl entered the yeshiva at noon and said that Mirele, long life to her, was beside herself with worry, and wanted to know how he was doing. "How are you, my son?" Brayndl asked.

"I'm better," he replied. "If it hadn't been for your daughter taking pity on me, I don't know what would have happened. She saved me."

"She's a diamond of a child," Brayndl said with happy pride. "She doesn't have an angry bone in her body. Let God give her as much good luck as I've had in her. Pray to God for her; she is, poor thing, an orphan. May God reward her for her refined heart, and may God also give you what you wish for. Be healthy, my son."

On her way out, Brayndl told the yeshiva sexton to keep the chimney open so Hershele would not get sick again. But the sexton swore there had been no charcoal fumes—the proof, he said, was that none of the other boys had headaches.

"How can you compare Hershele to the others?" Brayndl asked. He is a genteel child, his head is not as stuffed-up as theirs. Pay attention, I beg you!"

"But he's had nothing in his mouth to eat today," said the sexton. "Do a mitzvah, Brayndl, don't stint with the *kasha* and butter—and make it fresh butter!"

A couple of hours later, Brayndl's maid brought a bowl of barley soup and hard bread to the study house along with cookies, tea, and sugar. She told Hershele—when no one was listening—

that the cookies, tea, and sugar were from Mirele, who bade him get well soon.

He hadn't eaten for two days and was happy for the soup which he ate down to the bottom of the bowl. He was even a little embarrassed in front of the serving maid, who waited for the bowl, afraid she might say he was eating like a healthy fellow.

But there was no need for Hershele to remain hungry. Shortly after the maid left, Borekh the butcher's wife arrived with a special meal for him. He had to invite a couple of the yeshiva boys to help him clean the plate.

THREE

Lying on the study house bench that night, no longer fainting from hunger or suffering from fantasies and foggy hopes, Hershele's heart felt both delighted and distressed by all that had happened earlier in the day. That same night, Mirele lay tossing and turning in her soft warm bed, also unable to sleep.

Her earlier feelings of fear and caring were reawakened. As soon as she closed her eyes to sleep, she saw Hershele lying pale on the sofa without his cap. She saw his dear, pale forehead, his lovely temples under his dark hair, his two big black eyes looking at her with thanks and asking her to show compassion for his poverty and loneliness.

She was embarrassed to be thinking of him and forced herself to banish the image from her mind. In humiliation, she turned her thoughts to her cousin Shmulke. She grew cold remembering her aunt's listing of Shmulke's fine traits and merits.

She closed her eyes harder and saw Hershele again. She saw him so close it seemed she could hear him breathing. Suddenly, she flung the pillows away, then gathered them around her again. She remembered his going off to the study house to sleep—sick, poor thing, on a hard bench without even a cushion. Her heart was flooded with pity; she wanted to know how he was doing. Did his head still hurt?

"Lonely Hershele," she thought. "If I weren't a girl I'd go see how you're doing even though it's the middle of the night. I'd bring you a cushion and a blanket and sit near you—the way a brother would—until you were feeling healthy again."

And it hurt her that she hadn't pressed him harder to stay the night; it hurt even more that she hadn't thought to send some little treat for him to eat that evening. She vowed to rise early in the morning and bring him whatever food she could find in the house. She lay there with such thoughts until the clock struck four and she finally fell asleep.

When she awoke, she found her mother had already finished praying and was eating breakfast. "What's the matter with you, my child?" Brayndl asked. "Why do you look so sad?"

Mirele was embarrassed and didn't know what to say, but since Brayndl was worried, she answered, "I must've caught Hershele's illness. My head hurts a bit and I didn't fall asleep until four."

Almost with a shout, Brayndl sent her daughter back to bed, and soon brought her tea, delicacies, and her best preserves.

"Nobody gives *him* anything, Mama," Mirele said with a sigh. "Isn't he a lonely fellow?"

"You see how precious a mother is to her child?" Brayndl replied. "As long as a mother lives, she takes care of her child like the eyes in her head. When a mother dies, God forbid, it's terrible for the orphan, poor thing. It's not just bad if he's far away—even in his hometown he's lonely as a stone."

"It's a good deed, Mama, to take pity on the forlorn," Mirele said. "You should have pity on him, too. My heart goes out to him, lying there sick without even a pillow, no faithful hand to bring him something. He's surely had nothing to eat today."

Brayndl wasn't surprised by her daughter's compassion; she'd always praised her for her good heart. And even Brayndl herself had often felt sympathy for Hershele—though she'd never done anything about it. She knew that compassion was a virtue in a maiden of marriageable age, and she gazed with love at her only child who possessed such fine qualities.

She promised Mirele she'd go to visit the sick boy; and if he were still too sick to go for his charity meal, she'd come home and send something to make him feel better. Why drag herself all the way to the yeshiva with a bowl of food when it might not be necessary? And the serving maid needed to stay home with Mirele, who was not feeling well herself.

A few minutes later, Brayndl headed off to the study house. When she returned home, she brought the news to Mirele: "Hershele can't forget your goodness in saving him from fainting. He was really, poor thing, strongly overcome by charcoal fumes and still isn't feeling well."

From that Wednesday on, Mirele began to feel shy in Hershele's company. If she knew he was in the house, she didn't come out of her room until she'd gone to the mirror, looked at herself, and combed her hair. Then she'd run through the dining room like the wind, enter the kitchen, and then swiftly return to her room.

FOUR

Poor Hershele lived through this time quite differently. As he recovered from his imaginary sickness, he felt almost happy. His heart was hopeful without knowing exactly what it hoped for. He knew he wanted to be rich, very rich, at least as rich as Rothschild. Then he'd give it all away, not saving the tiniest bit for himself. Mirele would thank him and he wouldn't be embarrassed any longer. He'd be able to talk with her as a brother talks with a sister; sing for her and she'd understand his singing. What more could he need from the world?

But how could this come about? How does someone in a poor study house become rich? And why would Mirele need his riches? She was already the richest girl in the town. Yet none of this worried him. If God wills it, even someone in the study house could become rich. Elijah the Prophet could come and reveal where a hidden treasure was buried. Why not? How could he be charming in Mirele's eyes if not with gold, silver, and precious stones? How could he come to her without Rothschild's riches? He begged God, "Make me rich through a miracle." He'd been serving God with his whole heart; didn't he deserve it?

When the next Wednesday rolled around again and it was time to return to Brayndl's for his meal, it suddenly occurred to him how tattered and poor his clothes looked. He thought how pathetic he must appear in her eyes and was embarrassed by his appearance.

It was clear that God didn't want to perform a miracle for him. Elijah, no doubt aware of the pain in his heart, didn't want to make him happy. It was already noon and he had to go eat. Though he'd rather fast for three days than go ragged and pitiful to Brayndl's, he could not avoid it. Refuse her weekly meal? How could he do that?

So he went, not for the meal but to see Mirele, even if only a glimpse from afar. It tugged at him; he couldn't find any peace, but he had to go. He had to see her.

He washed himself in the basin of the study house and took a good look at himself in the water as if it were a mirror. He combed his black curly hair, set his cap on his head just so, and headed out for his meal.

And so it went on the following week and the week after that. His heart suffered terribly and he found no means to become rich and happy.

One day he came across a little book that had no cover. He started reading it by accident, but after just a few pages he couldn't let it out of his hands. It had within it such sweet thoughts, lovely expressions, and beautiful language, that seemed to have come directly from his own heart.

It was titled *Love of Zion,* and at first he was not afraid to open it in the presence of the Gemara—he didn't know that the little book was one of those forbidden, demonic works which the apostate Akher drew out of his breast. But Hershele didn't find a single heretical word in it; on the contrary, everything he read reminded him of the holy land, *Eretz Yisroel.* The grand and beautiful city of Jerusalem seemed to stand before him so realistically. He could see her as if he were standing within her. He saw Yedidya the nobleman; he saw the sons of the prophets, and the Temple Mount. He stood on the Mount of Olives and saw the fearsome Dead Sea from afar. He loved reading it in Hebrew, the language of sanctity, though it was not poetry, Gemara, or the Zohar.

Why wasn't he born in that blessed time? He would've talked with Mirele in the holy tongue. He would've been a shepherd, shot a wolf or some other wild beast with an arrow, and saved her from death. Where, he wondered, was the heresy in that?

But later he hid the book, afraid that people would discover how his heart suffered for Mirele. The writer, like a prophet who knows everything, had looked into his heart and told its secret in the love story of Amnon and Tamar, though he is called Hershele and she Mirele.

He memorized the little book's fine words; and when Mirele came into his mind while reading, his lips would whisper in Hebrew, "my dove, my heart's desire, delicate one of my heart," and it pained him that Mirele knew nothing of the holy tongue. If she understood Hebrew, he thought, he would let himself be captured, carried away, and sold as a slave in the great city of Nineveh. There he would rest on the grass in the vineyard and write her a letter just as Amnon wrote to Tamar. He would cherish the pain of captivity as long as Mirele read his letter.

These dreams, however, made him happy only while his eyes were buried in the book. When he looked up at the dark, dusty study house and saw the muddy floor and the long burnt table, greasy with tallow candle wax, he felt himself even poorer and more desolate than before. Finally he admitted to himself that a happy Amnon could only exist back then while Isaiah the Prophet was alive, Jews still lived in the land of *Yisroel,* and milk and honey flowed in the streets. Now, he thought, living among gentiles with *Shekhinah* no longer resting upon us, women don't understand even one word of Hebrew.

"No," he told himself, "neither a letter like Amnon's nor a song like the one he sang to Tamar will help me find favor or respectability in Mirele's eyes. Somehow I must get rich, as rich as Rothschild, as rich as Montefiore. But how?"

Lying on a bench in the yeshiva, thinking about where to find a hidden treasure, he scolded himself: "No, no treasures. The Gemara says one must not long for miracles. One must do what one can, really work hard, and expend strength and health to bring oneself up in the world. I must study night and day until I become an important scholar, a great wise man. Then she'll know I'm respectable."

Later that night he got up and studied with burning diligence until morning. When it was time, he prayed with great piety and fervor. He also began to fast whenever he could find the slightest justification. And so he studied, prayed, and fasted for a whole month; and people, delighted by his diligence and praising him for his piety, didn't notice Hershele growing paler and weaker, his cheeks sunken, his eyes dull, and his expression without a trace of happiness in it.

Only the head of the yeshiva, who loved him like a son, observed the change in him, but he also knew that studying Torah could exhaust a man and recalled the Gemara's pronouncement that one cannot know Torah without beating oneself black and blue in the study house. He believed that Hershele could become a magnificent scholar and so allowed him to study as much as his heart desired.

Nobody, perhaps not even Hershele himself, understood his burning fire for Torah, which sapped his youthful strength and enveloped his world in such bitter smoke. He had completely stopped singing, and though his friends often asked, "Hershele, please sing something; it's so sad in the study house when you don't sing," he always replied, "Singing is from the Evil Inclination. I wish I weren't able to sing. Singing brings pain to the heart!"

He never forgot Mirele—but the more he thought of her, the more diligent and pious he became. If he'd been able to find a good reason, one that wasn't a lie, he'd have fasted on Wednesdays and not gone to Brayndl's for his meal.

Once, finding Brayndl away from the house again, he decided to leave without eating. What would he do if Mirele showed up while he waited; pretend to be overcome by charcoal fumes again? But before he could turn and go, he heard a sweet voice coming from Mirele's room, a moving melody sung with such feeling it grabbed his heart. He stood transfixed, as if the voice nailed him to the spot. He quickly realized it was Mirele who was singing; and though he knew the Gemara warned against the sinfulness of a woman's voice and that he himself was sinning by just listening, he couldn't find the strength to leave. She sang on until he forgot where he was, until, without realizing it, he had joined quietly into the melody with her.

He couldn't move even when the voice stopped; it seemed he could still hear the song. Suddenly the door opened and Mirele was standing before his eyes.

"Oh, Hershele," she said in a friendly manner. "So you heard me singing. Did I sing well?"

"Very well," he replied, "but please don't be offended that I listened."

"They say you are a very good singer, too," Mirele said excitedly. "Is it true? Did you study singing?"

"When would I have time to study singing?" he asked.

"Why don't you have the time?"

"I must study; that's the main thing. Singing is just whatever it is."

Mirele, feeling a bit deflated by his answer, looked at him with embarrassment. He dropped his eyes.

"Sit down," she said, "why are you standing?"

"It's time to go back to the study house."

"Why hurry? Have you eaten yet?"

"I don't want to eat. Good day."

"Hershele, why don't you want to talk with me?" Mirele asked.

Reluctantly, Hershele sat down and waited for her to begin.

"Tell the truth," she said, "do you really not have time, or do you not want to be here alone with me?"

"I really don't have time," he answered, trembling and embarrassed.

"What is it you have to do?"

"I have to study."

"Tell me, why do you study so much? They say you study all the time, day and night. You don't eat, you don't sleep, you only study. Is that a good way for things to be?"

He looked at her and his eyes asked, "Do you mean to distract me from the holy Torah?" She understood his look and quickly replied, "Don't think I'm asking you not to study—study, but just take care of your health. A person must also be healthy, and you are not well. Does everyone study as much as you do?"

"If I don't study more than the others, I won't understand more than they do. But I also want to know more; I have to know more, and that's why I slave away."

"Why?"

"Because I want to be respected; I want to be a great scholar."

"And what will happen when you're a great scholar?"

"I'll be able to do good for the people who are helping me now."

"Who's helping you now? Who's worrying about you? Nobody is concerned that you are growing weaker every day. People are pleased by your scholarship and don't care that Torah is taking away your health. Everyone praises you for your singing, but no one is concerned with your loneliness. It's not worth it, I tell you, to sacrifice your health for the sake of some pitiful bits of bread you're given—people do it more for the mitzvah than for your thanks."

"So should I then not thank my friends for their generosity, which is dearer to me than my health?"

"Tell me, who are these friends?" she asked, moved by the deep truth expressed in his words.

"Have I no one, then, who's my friend? Who wishes me well and does kind things for me?" Hershele glanced at her as if to say, "Aren't you exactly the friend for whose sake I wish to become an important person?"

Mirele felt his gaze and dropped her eyes. "You have a friend," she said after a few moments of thought. "But it's not your thanks or your good works that she wants. This friend wants only for you to be healthy, and not downcast, and not embarrassed to look her in the eye. That would make her happy."

He looked at her, amazed and bashful; he didn't know if he'd heard this for real or in a dream.

"What do you say?" she asked, trying to get at least one word out of him.

"I don't deserve your kindness."

"Hershele, tell me you'll take care of your health. Then you'll not only have my kindness but also my friendship."

"Tell me, what should I do? I want to obey you in every way; I know you want only the best for me."

"Just your health, nothing more. Believe me."

And she really had no other motive. His pallor tore her heart to pieces, and she thought it was his loneliness that made him seem so lovable and unforgettable.

She went to the kitchen and prepared a meal for him with her own hands. He ate, though he didn't need to; he felt filled up by her kind words.

Before he left she gave him a few rubles towards the expense of regaining his health. "I don't need any money," he said, not wanting to take it. "I'm not lacking for my daily meals."

"You once gave me to understand you wanted to be rich," she said. "It's just a loan in case you need some clothes. I worry about you; take it for my sake. If you don't, it will be a sign you don't believe me and that my friendship is worth nothing to you."

Without any more objections, he took the rubles.

FIVE

The morning after that happy Wednesday was the first day of the month and "Happy Adar!" was heard throughout the study house. In Hershele's heart there was also a celebration: sweet hopefulness arose and danced before his eyes. He prayed and sang quietly, lovingly; he looked at the sun as it melted the snow and ice, and he felt a warm sun shining inside himself, melting the heavy stone that had been pressing on his heart. He felt warmed, even happy.

A few of the schoolboys closed their Gemaras as the end of the term approached. Even the head of the yeshiva reminded Hershele there'd be no harm in studying a little less. "You've slaved away enough for one semester," he said. "Now you should be satisfied to study all day and a couple of hours at night and then sleep like everyone else. One needs to consider one's health too, my son. We don't have the strength of King David, who would catch just a wink of sleep, then rise again to do God's work like a lion."

Hershele obeyed him and began to sing again.

One of the schoolboys, who also had a lovely voice, concocted a plan: since the end of the semester would occur around Purim, it would make sense to put on a *Purimshpiel,* a Purim play, of "King Saul" or "The Selling of Joseph."

"People should know," he said, "that we can do more than just study something the well-off householders' donkey sons can't do!"

All the schoolboys seized on this immediately. Almost all of them knew the melodies. The head of the yeshiva soon consented, and after plenty of effort and persuasion, the town's rabbi also agreed, under the conditions that all proceeds go to charity and that no women be allowed into the study house.

Nobody quarreled with the first condition but they protested the second. They finally agreed the ban on women wouldn't be strongly enforced if it came to a test.

At first Hershele didn't want to participate in the play; he thought Mirele would be offended seeing him as a *Purimshpieler.* But his friends insisted: he was their great hope; it wouldn't work without him.

"You must play Joseph," they declared, "nobody else can handle this difficult role. And how can you shirk when your friends need you?"

After plenty of argument, Hershele finally consented and took on the task, not only of learning his own role, but of coaching his friends in their parts as well. A few days later, the roles had been assigned and the study house was full of singing. Hershele directed and everyone obeyed him.

For three rubles in cash, Yosl the ragman had lent them old officers' and generals' uniforms, sabers, and helmets. The boys went up to the women's section, locked the door, and took to measuring the clothes. Hershele received an old general's uniform, so broad and long he was lost in it. The other schoolboys, however, were proud of their military uniforms and showed a proud spirit, imagining themselves with chests high and daggers in hand, heroes prepared to fight to the death.

Suddenly, while looking over his cast, Hershele announced, "I think we're missing something. These clothes are completely wrong for our play."

"What?" surprised voices called out from all sides.

"Who were Joseph's brothers?" he asked. "Shepherds! How does a shepherd come by epaulets and watch chains? We should be dressed in simple shepherds' clothes with long sticks and rough sacks. The Ishmaelites should walk with bound heads, like the Turks. Only in Egypt, when the brothers come to visit Joseph, should the guards standing by the throne be dressed in officers' clothing, because that's suitable for palace guards."

A great argument broke out with everyone refusing to accept Hershele's crazy plan. "From the beginning of time," they protested, "'The Selling of Joseph' has been played in officers' clothing. How will it look if we are dressed as simple shepherds? A travesty!"

Trying to win them over, he offered to pay a ruble and twenty kopecks of his own money to buy new clothes, including a robe with a silk girdle for himself, just the way he wanted it. And he was pleased to find a pair of long, skin-colored stockings so he wouldn't be completely barelegged.

The son of Ben-Zion the shopkeeper was allowed to attend rehearsals under the condition that he bring with him various things they needed. He was so happy to be the only *cheder* boy allowed to enter, he brought even more than they asked for. His mother gave him some things, others he simply stole from the store. Other boys pitched in as well, and in the end, nothing was lacking.

The most beautiful clothes were chosen for Hershele, and a few tailors' apprentices mended and altered the clothes to fit. They also used shirt silk to create a wonderful coat of many colors. Other boys prepared bows and arrows, shepherds' bags, and decorated little pitchers with birch bark.

The brave spirit which seized them the first time they were measured for the military uniforms wasn't lost. They hoped to show their heroics later when Joseph would recognize them and make them princes in the land of Egypt—especially the boy playing Judah, who had from the very beginning been allowed to wear epaulets and a watch chain because he was the leader of all the brothers.

Of course, nothing proceeds without aggravation, and Hershele worried that the yeshiva space was too small to perform the comedy. The *bimah* platform took up much of the room and there was nowhere to stage the play except where the audience should sit. Though they measured and planned, the place was just too small. They wracked their brains to find a suitable space until God took pity on them and provided someone to save the day.

Avreml the baker lived near the yeshiva; he had a big house and every year he baked matzah for the whole town. He even sent matzah to Moscow and Saint Petersburg. At Purim, he always emptied the house and prepared the tables and baking tools for Passover. The house was already empty, and it fell to Hershele to ask Avreml if he would consider letting them use his house in exchange for a small fee. He bargained with the baker all night, offering him their last few coins. A few schoolboys, who were good matzah-rollers, even promised their help at Passover. In the end, Avreml agreed to let them stage their *Purimshpiel* in his house.

Fortunately, there was no lack of lumber, and the boys spent the next few days and nights building a stage for the actors and benches for the guests. Once everything was completed, there was another celebration.

Just before Purim, tickets were distributed with the seal of the charity hospital printed on them. Sixty rubles were collected, and the head of the hospital gave twenty-five of them to the yeshiva for an end of term feast. The rest were added to the charity's coffers.

The whole town considered this event a great marvel. Once a year at a fair, a person could see a juggler with a glass of water on his forehead twist himself through a hoop without spilling a drop, but a play with singing had never been seen in the town. Therefore, wives and maidens loudly grumbled over the rabbi's sanction against allowing women to see the play. "Our souls aren't raisins," they complained. "Are we so sinful we can't watch the brothers throwing Joseph into the pit of snakes?"

The rabbi was finally won over by his daughter-in-law, and it was decided that the benches would be divided, men on the south side and women on the north, and the audience would go in and out through two different doors to prevent any mingling.

Hershele and the other boys worked the whole day to move the benches and make a dividing curtain between the men and women's sections. By the time they had finished, he was exhausted and his heart ached; he regretted having let himself be convinced to participate in the show. He was sure he would not sing well; and if Mirele attended and he saw her from the stage, he feared his voice would crack or he would mix up his lines, and he would surely freeze up from embarrassment.

Though he had once wished Mirele could hear him sing, he now hoped she'd stay away so he wouldn't shame and degrade himself in her eyes. The schoolboys were distressed when they saw him yawning and acting so weary. "What's the matter, Joseph?" they asked; they were all using their characters' names so as not to forget them.

"If I could, I'd sleep until tomorrow," he answered.

"That can't happen!" they replied. "People are already gathering for evening prayers."

"And what about the food and the roast geese?" said another. "The head of the yeshiva's wife and the rebbetzin have been slaving away since last night."

"Hershele," they shouted at him, "talking like that is a sin. The show must go on!" Although he didn't feel well, they insisted acting wouldn't do him any harm. "Just remember, this is a graduation and money for the charity hospital," they told him. "Don't be afraid; as it is written, 'The bringer of a good deed is not harmed.'"

By evening the yeshiva was packed. The finest householders gathered, dressed in their best holiday clothes. There were candles burning in all the chandeliers. In the women's section, the rebbetzin and the esteemed women gathered. Young women were there, too, many for the first time, and the older wives called them to the windows saying, "Look, see the honor of the holy Torah."

The head of the yeshiva sat in the place of honor at the big table, which today for the first time was covered with a white tablecloth. On one side, the yeshiva boys sat by their open Gemaras; on the other side, the rabbi sat by the esteemed householders. Hershele sat at the place of honor, beside the head of the yeshiva, because he'd always been favored over the other boys.

Mirele sat in the women's section with her mother and looked down at him. His face was pale; only his eyes shone, as if lit by a fire. She didn't want to look at him, but couldn't resist.

One by one, the head of the yeshiva called his students, asking each to present his lesson. Some recited well, others stumbled. Hershele came last and for the first time Mirele heard how well he spoke; how sharply and distinctly each word came from his mouth.

When the rabbi asked him a question, Hershele's eyes sparked and he quickly found the answer. Heartened, he reasoned through the rest of his portion of the Gemara. The head of the yeshiva conducted a very thorough examination, which fascinated the men while the women yawned over the incomprehensible words.

The graduation ended with the serving of brandy and cakes. As the celebration concluded, the sexton called out, "Let it be proclaimed that those who have not bought tickets shall not be admitted to see "The Selling of Joseph"; to do so would be robbing from a charitable organization. And we ask that women not mix with the men."

The crowd bustled from the yeshiva to the theater at Avreml the baker's house, and there was a lot of wall-thumping before everyone settled down and the chatter was quieted. When the curtain finally went up, the audience saw Jacob Our Father sitting on the stage wrapped in a Turkish shawl and wearing a big flaxen beard. His son Joseph was stretched out beside him with his head on his father's lap. Jacob began to sing:

> Rise up from your sleep, my dear child.
> Go to your brothers.
> I'm sending you quickly.
> Bring me a message early tomorrow.
> About their health, about their cattle.

The voice was scratchy and hoarse; it tore your ears to hear it. Joseph rose, as if from sleep, like a yielding child. He sat himself at Jacob's right hand and, playing with his father's long beard, sang out his dream in a soft childish voice: how the sun, moon, and eleven stars bowed down to him. His voice and all his movements surprised everyone; and even before he finished, hundreds of hands were applauding from both the men and women's sections. Everyone wanted to know, "Who is this Joseph; who is this actor?"

The whispering quieted down when Jacob, in his hoarse voice, replied angrily to his child: "And will I, with your mother and brothers, come bow down to you? Your mother is dead!"

"My dear young mother is dead," Joseph began to sing a song of great sadness. Even sadder was the final scene, in which Jacob and his dear Joseph studied Torah and said farewell. Men in the audience listened earnestly; the women sobbed.

Little by little, Hershele was drawn more deeply into his role until he no longer saw the audience or cared who was there and who was not. And it wasn't only Hershele; the audience believed everything was really happening there before them. When the brothers shouted, "Here comes the dreamer!" and tore Joseph's silk coat, many in the audience felt their hearts being torn.

In that very moment, Hershele stood confused and surprised, looking at his brothers in wonder, as if he didn't understand them, or didn't know why they were so angry with him. But when they began to push him back and forth, he suddenly understood they were serious. With a moving melody he began to beg them for compassion; he pleaded with them to have mercy for his young years, and to take pity on their old father who would not survive the sorrowful news.

But this only made their anger grow wilder and more violent. "Kill him," they shouted. "Kill him, tear him to pieces, throw him into a hole!"

And so before his impending death, Hershele bade farewell to his brothers, the bright sun in the sky, and the happy and beautiful world. He prayed to God to console his father and forgive his sinful brothers.

Meanwhile, Jacob's oldest brother Reuben entered. To avoid the spilling of blood, he proposed that Joseph be thrown into the pit of snakes. Agreeing, the brothers quickly carried Hershele to the pit and threw him in. The audience gasped; would the snakes and lizards touch his skin with their poison?

Of course, everyone quickly realized the "pit" on stage was only a trunk without a bottom—not only lacking water, but also snakes and lizards. Nevertheless, when the brothers thrust Hershele into it, many cried out "Oy!" in terror.

Mirele, too, grabbed her heart and almost shrieked with sorrow. A heavy anxiety lay on the entire audience.

Joyfully, the brothers sat down to eat and drink. Suddenly, from the other side of the stage, a band of Ishmaelites arrived, their heads bound with red scarves and speaking an odd sort of Turkish. A deal was quickly struck, and the Ishmaelites unbound their girdles and paid with twenty silver coins. Then they pulled the pale, frightened Joseph from the snake pit with a rope, lashed him with whips, and drove him towards the back of the stage as the curtain came down.

As the curtain rose on the third act, the audience saw a path leading through a field; a band of Midianites slept on the ground snoring loudly. Joseph lay awake nearby. His hands were bound with chains and his head rested on a stone. Slowly he lifted his head and looked at a small hill on the other side of the path.

"What do my eyes see?" he asked quietly. "A tombstone with Jewish letters!" On hands and knees he crawled to the tomb and read the words aloud, "Here lies the woman—the wife of Jacob, son of Isaac, son of Abraham." Suddenly he cried out, "My mother's tomb!"

He remained quiet for a very long time, as if the air were too heavy to breathe, and Hershele felt as if he were no longer on stage acting, but there in the tiny forsaken village graveyard where his own dear mother rested. And how his heart longed to see her grave again, to moisten the earth with his tears. He stood there yearning to tell her his pain, his secrets, which only a mother would understand. Perhaps she could go to God now and intercede for him and for Mirele, who sat so close and yet so far away.

He spread his chained hands and embraced the tombstone the way an unhappy child goes to be soothed by his devoted mother. Then he sang with a sob in his voice:

> To your grave, mother,
> He throws himself at your feet.
> Recognize your Joseph, your trembling son!
> Your child, who you bore with pain,
> Your son, who lost you so early.
> My life is bitter and terrible, Mama.
> I've been sold for a slave.
> How can you see and hear this, Mama,
> That your dear Joseph shall be a slave?
> Rise quickly from your tomb, mother,
> Go petition God on behalf of your child.
> Let Him see my desolation, hear my pain.
> Return me to my beloved father,
> Or take me into your grave.
> I bitterly pour out my heart to you,
> I plead upon your holy grave.
> My heart remains with you, Mama.
> You know my desolation,
> You understand my heart's pain.
> Answer, mother, answer me,
> Or take me with you.

The more he sang, the more his constricted heart opened, and the deeper and more moving his voice became. Suddenly, he saw

Mirele seated with her mother on the first row. All his pain and suffering poured forth in the words of the song. His voice was sweet and tender, and real tears—not theater tears—poured down his burning cheeks. Nearly everyone in the audience wept with him— but none knew the true source of his tears.

When the Midianites, duly scratching, awoke from their sleep, they began to laugh and make fun of Joseph for sobbing and talking to a stone. Joseph didn't turn around, but as they came to him, there was a cry from the tomb.

"Mother, mother," he shouted so realistically it jolted everyone's heart. Some men, overcome with pity, rose from their benches with clenched fists, ready to run and save Joseph from the wild Midianites. On the women's side a wailing and lamenting arose as in the women's section during Yom Kippur prayers.

A voice called out from the tomb:

> I have heard your wailing, my child,
> You are blessed by a beloved God.
> Your dreams shall be realized,
> And you will go back to your people.
> God will repay you for your pain,
> And the luckiest of women will be yours!

Hearing the voice of Rachel, Joseph's dead mother, helped to calm the audience. Clenched fists opened and men sat back on their benches; women began to dry their eyes. Then, with a great outcry from the Midianites, Joseph was surrounded and pushed towards the farthest depth of the stage. As the curtain closed, there was a storm of bravos: "Bravo, Joseph; bravo, Hershele!"

Old women begged, "Come, show us your bright face; let us see pride coming from sorrow." As people cheered, Hershele came out from behind the curtain and stood on the stage. Embarrassed, he bowed to the right and the left. Then he bowed to Mirele, and, as their eyes met, a thousand thanks, a thousand blessings, and a thousand secrets passed between them.

A half hour later, Rachel's stone tomb was transformed into Pharaoh's palace of whitewashed boards. Mirele sat as in a dream, distracted, not even sure of her own thoughts. She awoke when a young woman sitting behind her whispered in her ear, "Oy, Mirele, I faint. I'd like to kiss all his limbs. See how beautiful he is!"

Mirele lifted her eyes to the stage and saw a young man in a finely fitting general's uniform. He stood leaning on his shield with pride and virtue. She had to look hard to see that this was the same Hershele. Even in her dreams, she had never seen him so majestically handsome.

His commanding tone with his attendants, his clever speech with his brothers, all his movements and gestures were so natural, it was as if he really was the mighty general in whose clothes he shone. With her eyes glued to him standing there like a king among his servants, she forgot this was the same Hershele whose poverty and loneliness had broken her heart. At this moment, she wanted to be richer and more beautiful than she actually was; she felt too poor and unworthy to dream of being his beloved. "It's good I didn't wait until now to offer my friendship," she thought. "I know he won't forget."

It didn't surprise Brayndl that her dear child was looking so dreamy and sad; other girls were also showing red eyes after the earlier scenes. Even she had held a handkerchief to her eyes on several occasions during the performance. Was it any wonder her always good and sympathetic Mirele was so moved and saddened by the play?

"Mirele," she consoled her daughter, "now you should be happy; God didn't fail. See Joseph's greatness, his palace, his golden throne. See his handsome face; it shines like the bright sun in heaven. A marvel so great his brothers don't even recognize him." Mirele saw everything and truly recognized Hershele for the very first time.

"It's no wonder," a young wife said, "that Potiphar's wife fell in love with him and that the women slicing oranges cut their fingers looking at his beauty. One can hardly look at him. What a sight, what a person!"

When the last act ended, men hurried up onto the stage to thank Hershele, to press his hand and kiss him. In the women's section, Mirele heard a young woman say to her friend, "I am so jealous of the one who will marry such a beautiful man."

"My father-in-law, let him be healthy, was right not to want women to see this," said the rabbi's daughter-in-law to Brayndl after hearing the young woman's wanton talk, though even she herself could not get her fill of watching Joseph, who had come down from the stage and was receiving kisses from the head of the yeshiva and the householders for his good acting and even more for his lovely singing.

"Come home already," said an annoyed mother as she took her daughter by the hand. "What is there still to see here? You've seen and heard enough."

A few minutes later, the yeshiva's sexton called out, "All women, and anyone who doesn't have business here, please go home."

"Oy, our bad luck," one woman complained. "We go to the market, we buy the food, we work ourselves to death cooking; and yet when it comes to enjoying the feast, they tell us to go home."

But the rebbetzin replied, "It's not for nothing the men say the blessing, 'Rather than be a woman, better not to be born at all.' Come women, come along." Reluctantly, the women obeyed and made their way out of the theater.

The next week proved the rabbi had been right. Just as the Egyptian daughters once crept to the market to see their new and handsome viceroy, many of the town's maidens turned their wiles and strategies towards seeing the new Joseph and getting to know him better. Mirele's acquaintances wasted hours with her, apparently for the sake of friendship, but really with the hope of seeing him at her house on Wednesday.

But Hershele didn't come. The head of the yeshiva's wife had made a second banquet for the schoolboys from the leftovers of the previous night's feast, and Hershele couldn't leave to go for his Wednesday meal at Brayndl's.

Not expecting him to arrive, Mirele asked herself, did she really know him? Is he really as lovely as he looked in the theater? She understood why her friends sought her out, and now jealousy was added to her other emotions from the previous night. She was glad Hershele had not come for his meal.

The next day, Borekh the butcher's daughter laid a little note under Hershele's plate:

> I love you like my own soul.
> If you love me too, I'll be good to you.
> From me, your loving Soreh-Feyge Tabukhov
> P.S. Please tear up this note and don't show it to anyone.

Hershele didn't understand what she wanted from him. "Is she making fun of me?" he wondered. Angered by such impudence, he tore the note into tiny pieces. But as he left, Soreh-Feyge was waiting for him in the foyer.

"What do you say, Hershele?" she asked in a breathless voice, as if afraid.

"This is inappropriate," he answered turning to the door.

But she took his hand and swore it was all true—and that her father would agree, because he, too, loved Hershele. Confused and embarrassed, Hershele could barely hear what she whispered, and ran from the house like a thief.

"A new Evil Inclination; a new problem for me," he told himself. "The story of Joseph is going to play out for me in every detail. And now, of all things, a Potiphar's wife in Borekh the butcher's daughter, Soreh-Feyge!"

He thought all night about what he should do; how he could get out of this. Should he stop going to eat at Borekh's? Might Soreh-Feyge, in anger, think up some slander against him? If she did, Borekh would certainly believe her and take vengeance against him like Potiphar did against Joseph.

But what terrified him most was not Borekh's vengeance, but the idea that Mirele might find out. His angel, his dearest soul! How will he ever tell her this is only slander, a total lie?

The problem darkened the bright hopes that had been kindled in his heart when he distinguished himself in front of all the householders—and especially in front of *her*.

The next morning, after prayers, an unfamiliar boy handed Hershele a note and quickly ran away. After putting away his prayer shawl and *tefillin,* he sat down to read it:

To that wunnerful stage individual—that is, actor—who played Joseph. I have the honnor to enform you, respktid gentlman, that your acting on the stage was highly pleasing to myself. And your singing—such singing would make famous the greatest actors at the greatest concerts! I send you my thanks for much plezhur which you have give me, that is, that I had while I heard you and also saw you.

I hope of your genteele heart feeling, that you will pardon me that I, though a fraulein, write to you, although you have with me no acquaintenance. In the big city where I've been it's the fashion that even a fraulein can also touch on and notice great talents which the local people don't understand, don't like to notice and pay attention to you, and don't have the heart for to understand your exceellent feeling.

Also my genteel sir, you should understand, that it isn't just anybody who iss writing to you. You should want to know who is wishing you happiness and great succiss and all good things, from a wholly deep heart, should you be so good as to go walking on Shabbes in the evening to the bridge yull see a fraulein with a white shawll and with a white feather on her hat and with gloves and when she stops when she sees you that will be I! In the theater when you were playing, I was the second one seeting down from my friend Miri, Brayndl's daughter, with a fan in my hand. Oh revoir, adeeyoo!

The note was not signed, and the message with all its mistakes vexed him. It seemed he was sinning in God's eyes just by reading it. Suddenly, he regretted ever being in the play. He remembered the Gemara said Joseph was punished with the temptation of Potiphar's wife because he was impressed with his own beauty. And Avisholem, son of David, stumbled over his long hair only because he curled and styled it in order to be charming. And although he, Hershele, had never boasted of his beauty, he had in fact curled his hair before going onstage, and had also taken pleasure looking in the mirror to see how fine he looked in the general's uniform.

"Who knows?" he said anxiously to himself. "One sin begets another. I could, God forbid, come to iniquity. And what would Mirele say? No, you are my angel, my Good Inclination! When I think of you, the Evil Inclination has no power!"

He didn't leave the study house during Shabbes. He studied diligently though it was the time of year when even a yeshiva student was permitted to go for a walk. Indeed, all his friends were off to the bridge to see ice breaking up, logs being dragged down the river, and houses being flooded. However, he didn't want to meet the mysterious "fraulein" who'd written him the note, and so remained in the yeshiva alone.

That night he sang the Psalm, "Blessed are the innocent," with a tune as sad as if the words of the passage expressed his heart's own wound. He was even sadder on the following Wednesday when he hoped to see Mirele again. Now that he finally had the courage to talk to her, even to sing for her, Mirele didn't come out of her room. It seemed that for some reason, she was angry with him. As Brayndl's serving maid Deborah put down his plate, she looked at him as if she wanted to shout in his ear: "I know you aren't here for the food, but for that 'fraulein!'"

As he was leaving, he was greeted by Brayndl, who was walking with Shlomo the matchmaker. When she saw Hershele, she asked if he'd received his meal. He felt she was bragging to Shlomo about providing charity meals to a yeshiva boy so he'd tell any future in-laws of her piety. It grew dark in the street for him, although the sun was shining brightly.

"Mirele is your sun," screamed his heart, "but she will soon be someone else's bride. Then you will never see the sunlight again."

Coming into the study house, he paced back and forth. Everything he saw was cold and sad. He wanted to sit and study, recite the Psalms, be as pious as he'd been before, but he could no longer understand the words of the Gemara. They swam before his eyes as in a sea of tears.

His friends all knew that Hershele's Joseph had stirred the hearts of the town's maidens. They were not all as naïve and guileless as he. In this yeshiva, as in others, students could be found who already carried a longing for love in their hearts. Perhaps it wasn't their fault; perhaps they hadn't chosen it. But they were at an age when romance comes uncalled and is often found even when it isn't sought.

A schoolboy's heart is filled with young blood; his life is awakening. The spring sun shines and sends a warm light over the world. Beautiful flowers of emotion sprout and quicken in hidden and forsaken corners exactly as they do in pretty, well-tended gardens. Nature is good to all her creatures and doesn't forget the rejected schoolboys who live their lives on the dry, hard benches of yeshivas.

But just as a forsaken and downtrodden flower quickly loses its spirit and beauty, a schoolboy's romance is often trampled down. Instead of improving him and making him a better man, it corrupts his innocence and health.

Among Hershele's friends, there were a few who'd caused him plenty of suffering, though he tried to remain silent. Every day they'd bring him news about which girl was already in love with him and which girl had the intention of falling in love with him and were now seeking opportunities to meet him. These schoolmates gave Hershele advice and shared their experiences, explaining how to behave with girls and properly turn their heads.

When Hershele would redden with indignation, they laughed at him and called him "prideful" and "a hypocrite" for his seeming lack of interest. He had only one consolation: the section in the Gemara that warned against evil speech. He saw no sin in his longing for Mirele so long as he remained silent.

But the schoolboys began to quarrel about it. One boy said, "Be careful, Hershele. As the mother is greedy—may her name be blotted out—the daughter is too generous. As the mother begrudges a schoolboy a bit of bread, the daughter doesn't begrudge any boy a good look. To the devil with her and her mother!"

"Listen, Hershele," said another, "she's the prettiest girl in town and also the richest. If I'd been eating for a whole year at Brayndl's house, had your voice and your charm, and distinguished myself the way you did playing Joseph, there'd be no doubt she'd have fallen for me. Be a man, take her. Just remember, don't be prideful and forget who gave you this great advice."

"Stupid, empty words," said a third boy. "One is forbidden to measure himself too high. Hershele could fall and break his neck."

"How do you know that?" replied the other boy. "From what evidence do you infer that she's not already in love with him?"

"I'll tell you how I know she's already in love with him," said the second boy who began a Gemara-like reply: "I deduced it from 'the more so' and 'by analogy.' If a complete stranger of a girl, seeing you for the first time, not knowing your fine qualities, loses her head and her heart to you when she sees you playing the Viceroy of Egypt, then Brayndl's daughter, who sees you every Wednesday, and whose mother, a shrew of a woman, can't stop praising your gifts and your charms, one can plainly see 'the more so': Mirele must love you.

"'By analogy' provides even more proof. Let's take singing for instance. I don't want to be too explicit and give away her name, but let's just say, for example, Borekh the butcher's daughter has fallen head over heels in love with you and nearly dies whenever she thinks of your name. And why? Because she has a feeling for good singing. Therefore, similarly, when Brayndl's only daughter, who has an even finer feeling for singing, hears your magnificent voice, she is certainly guaranteed to love you just as the other one does, whose name I may reveal to you in the future."

These two arguments pleased all the boys in the yeshiva, and it was agreed that Brayndl's daughter was in love with Hershele, but that he was a fool and would certainly pay a sinner's price if he didn't properly become Brayndl's son-in-law with a betrothal and wedding canopy according to the laws of Moses. "What do you say, Hershele?" they all asked him.

Hershele could hardly believe what he had heard; his face reddened, then blanched. He seethed with fury at his friends' devilish words about Brayndl, and was incensed by their talk about Mirele, his sweet and delicate one, his light and sun. Yet he refused to let his heart's true secret be revealed by his anger; he bent his head down and didn't say a word. But the schoolboys pestered him, insisting on a reply.

It took Hershele a very long time to answer. Finally he said in a very quiet voice, "Should I be shameless and talk the way you do? It's bad enough that you say things that one should be ashamed of even thinking about—full of coarseness and obscenity—but that you also boast of it here in a holy place. You then slander the name of a Jewish daughter and goad me to follow in your ways."

"Fool, simpleton," one of the boys replied, but the others stood shamefaced and silent.

"Better I should be a fool than a bad person," Hershele said as he turned and walked away from them. Picking up a Gemara, he found a passage and read it silently to himself: "That man is good who does not follow the path of the wicked or place himself in the way of sin; who doesn't sit at the Council of Fools, passing time emptily and engaging in mockery. What then does he do? His desire is only in Torah and he burns for learning day and night."

With these words, he turned back to studying with the same intensity as before, hoping in this way he would be healed of both his open and hidden wounds.

SIX

Hershele didn't follow the path of the wicked and didn't place himself in the way of sin. He didn't join his devil-tongued schoolmates, but instead studied as before, day and night, until he could study no longer. The fire, which had burned quietly in his heart, grew as hot as the fire from Torah; in vain he sought to fight fire with fire.

At times he complained to his heart, "Why won't you let me rest? Aren't I charming and honored enough already? Aren't all my friends jealous of my name and my singing? What more do you want from me? I don't need anything else; not riches, not honors. Things are fine with me as they are. But you, heart, you keep longing for more and more. You're sick within me."

Another time, unintentionally remembering his friends' words, he asked himself, "Am I perhaps love-sick? Is this love? No, no! Love is sinful; it's of the Evil Inclination. I don't want from Mirele what my friends are talking about or what Borekh's daughter wants from me. I just want to see her again, hear her sing, talk with her, be close to her. I want to sing to her, day and night; happy songs and sad ones, too; I want to console her with my songs and make her cry. I want to wander with her somewhere in a deep and distant forest, where one sees no houses, no people, no roads, no paths, only trees, blossoms, mountains, valleys, rivers, and springs. I'd take her by the hand and tell her not to be afraid; I would do battle even with wild animals for her sake. I'd sit her on the soft grass; she'd be surrounded by flowers, and I'd collect wonderful fruit to refresh her. We'd never be hungry or thirsty, or lack for anything. And she'd tell me she always knew how faithful I was to her. This is all I need; I don't need anything more.

"So why is this a sin against God? Wouldn't she and I be devout and pious, praying and praising Him with our whole hearts for his benevolence in letting us be together? And why doesn't God sense my desire? Why would it trouble Him to make me happy?"

In this dreamy state he studied Gemara and recited Psalms without knowing what he studied or hearing what he said. Mirele had become dearer and dearer to him with each passing day although two Wednesdays had gone by since he'd last seen her.

One day while Hershele was sitting in this dreamy state, Shlomo the matchmaker came into the yeshiva and asked about his family. Where did he come from? Who was he related to? Was he registered for the draft?

"Why do you care about all this?" Hershele asked.

"You're a fool," Shlomo laughed. "Don't you know I'm a matchmaker?"

Hershele suddenly remembered he'd seen Shlomo walking with Brayndl and felt a stab in his heart. "I know you're a matchmaker," he said. "I even know you've found a match for Mirele, Brayndl's daughter. Tell me, Reb Shlomo, whom did you find for her? Is he a good man? Can he study? Does he like to sing?"

"What business is that of yours?" the matchmaker asked, looking him over.

"I need to know. I'll go to the bridegroom you've chosen for her and tell him there's no other bride in the whole world with as many virtues as Mirele."

Hershele believed this with his whole heart. Not having the slightest hope a matchmaker would propose him for Mirele, and not realizing what Mirele really meant to him, he wanted to be faithful and loving and at least show this lucky bridegroom what an angel he was getting.

"What do you mean?" the matchmaker answered with a smile. "Mirele's a girl like any other girl. You think they all have to be as beautiful and capable as she? You know what, I give a pinch of snuff for her superiority. I can tell you, Borekh the butcher's daughter will be a better wife and mother than Brayndl's Mirele."

Hershele looked at the matchmaker in disbelief. It hurt to hear his angelic Mirele compared to Borekh's common and vulgar daughter—a girl as much like Mirele as night is to day. How could Reb Shlomo not understand the difference?

"Listen, Hershele," said the matchmaker. "What's the point of talking about Brayndl's girl? Forget it, she's already got her bridegroom. It's not my concern and it's not your concern either. I've come with good news for you: Borekh the butcher wants you for his Soreh-Feyge. You know her, and let me tell you, may I have as many good years as you'll have with such a bride. I guarantee you'll come to appreciate her. Listen, Hershele, I know everything. I have eyes; one look and I see how things are. Be a man and know I want you to be happy. Honestly, this is happiness for you. And if I didn't know you're a pauper without a kopeck to your name, I'd ask you to buy me a glass of brandy to celebrate. But no matter, have a good day."

Hershele's heart seized up; he couldn't say a word. But Shlomo the matchmaker didn't need a reply. "Just know, this is your lucky day," Shlomo said. "And you yourself chose it. I heard the news you flirted with her; she told me this herself."

With these words, Shlomo was off to Borekh's house to say there'd been no difficulties, and to extol Hershele's virtues as well: "Besides his being a genius and besides all his other admirable qualities—one could search the whole world and not find such qualities in today's bachelors—he also comes from a very fine family: his father was a scholar and famous cantor in the Bednarker Kehilah, his grandfather on the other side was a judge, and his uncle is a rabbi in Dlutovsk to this very day.

"Besides all this, he is a diligent young man and realizes you do well by him. And he has eyes in his head; your Soreh-Feyge, may she be well, will please him. No disrespect, Reb Borekh, but you and I lived in different times. In our day, who even looked at the face, as long as it was a bride? Today, a modern boy looks at the face and you and your daughter have nothing to be embarrassed about. Give me as many years as she'll be a lovely bride!"

Borekh agreed to make the match and the two men drank a toast to the happy couple.

Hershele had remained alone in the yeshiva after the matchmaker left. Frightened, he asked himself, "What is this? Is he really talking about me? Be a bridegroom? Get married? And what of Mirele? No, she may marry, she must, but I can't. Not now. Even if Rothschild offered his daughter for a bride, I'd refuse him. Then again, could I ever forget Mirele? Never!"

That same day towards twilight, Borekh threw off his carcass-stained butcher's clothes, dressed up as respectably as he could, and headed to the study house for evening prayers. He wanted to ask the head of the yeshiva about the quality of Hershele's scholarship. He knew that in a field in which one is not an expert, it is important to seek outside opinions. Why not ask someone more clever and experienced? Especially when it comes to a match for your first-born child.

When Borekh saw Hershele in the study house, he spoke to him in a very gentle and amiable voice—not about the essence of the matter at hand, but with warmth—a warmth that turned Hershele ice-cold. Then he had a private chat with the head of the yeshiva.

The rebbe grumbled when he heard Borekh's question and curtly informed the butcher there was no boy in the whole school better than Hershele. Furthermore, the head of the yeshiva insisted, he would not let Hershele go unless all the circumstances were favorable for him.

"Hershele should come into a house where he will find people who truly appreciate him," said the rebbe. "I ask you, is it a match made in heaven? There are now—no evil eye—many who are eager for Hershele. You are not the first; a few well-to-do householders have already talked to me about this.

"If the match with your daughter is blessed by God, no one else will grab him. You don't have to worry someone else will get him first; that can only happen with a second marriage. As you know, in the case of a first marriage, forty days before the birth, a voice from heaven calls out the name of a person's *beshert*—his or her intended one. And why are you in such a hurry, Borekh?"

"Who's hurrying?" Borekh replied. "But why wait, Rebbe? It's time for my daughter to get married, and I feel sorry for him, the poor thing." The head of the yeshiva nodded his understanding.

"What do I know?" Borekh asked himself cheerfully as he left the study house. "He can beg for more—or I can even offer a little more. A match shouldn't be voided over a few hundred rubles lacking in the bride's dowry. As long as the transaction takes place, why haggle? She's my child, my crown. My boys are coarse, the devil's in their skins. Why shouldn't I have a little pride and pleasure from my daughter?"

The next day, Borekh headed to Brayndl's to arrange a loan. He'd always been her butcher, and in the past, he'd borrowed money from her to buy oxen. Coming into her house, he happily told Brayndl that the schoolboy, Hershele, who ate at her table on Wednesdays, would soon be Soreh-Feyge's bridegroom. "What do you say, Brayndl?" he asked. "Since you're a clever woman, let's hear your advice."

"There isn't another like him in all the world," Brayndl answered. "Have you ever seen such charm? Not to mention how easy he is on the eyes. What more could you ask for? My Mirele, let her be healthy, is so keen on him, she wouldn't trade him for a sack of onions. Since she heard him in 'The Selling of Joseph,' she can't stop singing his tunes. And his other good qualities: his skill at studying, his quietness, his refinement. You can even tell from the way he eats that he comes from a fine family. You know yourself it's a pleasure to host him for a meal. You'll have no large expenses with him, Reb Borekh; he's quite a bargain!"

That same day, after evening prayers, the head of the yeshiva invited Hershele to walk home with him for a cup of tea. Like a father, the good rebbe took the opportunity to compare Hershele's current condition as a poor schoolboy with what his life could be like as the son-in-law of Borekh the butcher: he'd have enough to eat and drink, no worries about livelihood, and, God willing, would be able to continue his studies. On the other hand, the rebbe pointed out, the Gemara says, "It's worth selling the shirt off your back to secure a wife whose father is a Talmud scholar."

As Hershele sat down at the table, the rebbe continued: "The holy Gemara says, cleverly and practically, that one who is coarse remains coarse. Children learn from their elders. It does sometimes happen that butchers, shoemakers, and tailors have intelligent children—but some vulgarity may still remain within them. We often see that grandchildren are like their grandparents. A person shouldn't feel, after living the good life for a while, that he's bought the world at too high a price. There are quite a few things to consider when one is contemplating marriage. Do you understand the essence of this wisdom of the Talmud, Hershele?"

Hershele was silent.

"Rebekah," the rebbe suddenly called to his daughter who was in the other room. "Bring us tea, my dear." A few minutes later, Rebekah came in, a maiden of about eighteen years, with beautiful black eyes. She offered two glasses of tea, shyly snuck a peek at the one-time Viceroy of Egypt, then quietly left the room.

"Drink, Hershele," the rebbe began again. "Now Borekh will, for example, treat you to kingly delights when he invites you to his home. I am a poor man, as you know. So you think, perhaps, I can't provide my daughter with a dowry? I'm not that poor, thank God. But let's lay that aside for now—though truly I respect you more than Borekh can—and return to the matter at hand: I say again, one must think very carefully and not immediately say 'yes' as soon as the matchmaker shows up with a prospect, or immediately say 'no' when the dowry is not as much as another might offer. The point is, my son, the principle involved. A kosher child, a daughter of fine parents, and not an unattractive girl; how is that bad? As our sages say, 'A beautiful bride.' Rebekah, why did you run away? Come back in here."

Rebekah returned to see what her father needed. The head of the yeshiva, however, had apparently forgotten why he just called her in, but let her stand there long enough for Hershele to have a look at his daughter as a truly beautiful bride.

But Hershele didn't look. He already knew Rebekah well; she was prettier, more pious, and cleverer than Borekh's daughter. But compared to Mirele?

Unsure of what the rebbe wanted, Hershele thought, "How I wish Mirele had such a good father, one who would talk to me so kindly." His heart hurt. He wondered why he and Mirele were fatherless orphans. He knew he'd never hear such kind words from her mother; as a woman, how could Brayndl speak with him so nicely? He sighed heavily.

"Don't worry, my son," the rebbe consoled him. "God, blessed be He, will show you the way. You're obliged merely to listen, to think it over, and to make up your own mind. It's no emergency, God forbid. What I wish for you I wish for me and my dear child as well."

The rebbe turned to Rebekah who was still standing there listening to her father's words. "I remember now," said the rebbe. "Bring us a bit of whiskey, my daughter." When she'd gone, he turned back to Hershele. "Tell me, have you perhaps cast your eye on Borekh's daughter? Does she perhaps please you more than any other? I don't want to dissuade you, understand, but there's really a big difference between me and Borekh. There's no point in my being overly modest, but on the other hand, perhaps Borekh's daughter is of a better sort than my child. These might be words of the heart which you're embarrassed to talk with me about. I tell you, Hershele, on my honor: although I wish all the best for my daughter, you are my dear student. I'm not trying to force your will—far from it."

"Rebbe," Hershele finally had the courage to answer. "What possible comparison can be made between you and Borekh, God forbid? You are a thousand times dearer to me than Borekh or any rich man. I don't want your dowry, I don't want your daughter.

Who's talking about marriage? I have no such intention—I want nothing to do with marriage. Please give me some advice, Rebbe. What answer can I give that won't make him my enemy?"

"Why are you afraid of him?"

"He's my patron; I eat a charity meal at his house once a week."

"What a child you are, Hershele. Borekh feeds you one meal a week; that's to say, he gives you an hour a day. And for that you don't have the heart to be ungrateful, though he proposes something you don't want? And yet with the one who has taught you Torah and shown you the way—you're not embarrassed to reject me and my daughter?

"Still, I have no complaint against you—I just want to point out that your reasoning has no foundation and no flavor. You say you don't want to marry, how can that be? Are you Ben Azzai, the famous celibate? Aren't we supposed to marry? How long do you propose to remain a bachelor? How long do you intend to eat a meal here, a meal there, and hang around the study house sleeping on a hard bench? And besides, the Gemara advises a Jew to be married at eighteen. It seems to me you must be about eighteen years old by now, right?

"And you think I want to drag you to the wedding canopy right away, God forbid? I think you should travel to Volozhin and study for another year. I'll see that you get a good letter explaining your circumstances, and, to the best of my abilities, I'll support you from home so you can study comfortably and achieve a good position.

"So the question is, why am I talking to you about this now? Don't I have plenty of time? The answer is, as the story goes: there are plenty of fathers who want you for their daughters. And Borekh, in particular, is in a hurry. He means to write a marriage contract as soon as the holidays are over. You, Hershele, are alone, with nobody to consult with you. Poverty and want influence the mind; I'm afraid you'll say a word you may later regret.

"I'll tell you how it looks to me, Hershele—but don't think I'm asking you to accept my opinion. If Borekh were a great householder and gave you a thousand rubles, or if he were at least a great aristocrat who could, even without the most lavish dowry, make you happy through family connections or a lucrative business, I'd be very happy for you and quickly give you my approval. But when all is said and done, he's just a butcher. Yes, a successful one, but what could he provide for you? In the best case, he could succeed in making you a partner in his business or possibly a land manager. I, too, could do as well for you by making you, with God's help, a cantor in this town or perhaps a bigger city somewhere else. Who knows, maybe you could become a rabbi or a judge—after all, are you a simpleton or a slacker in your studies? If it weren't for your one little defect of suddenly becoming distracted and dreamy, you have everything it takes to become a great teacher of Torah."

Hershele finally understood why his rebbe had wanted to talk with him. "He has always been so kind and faithful to me," he thought to himself. "How can I shame him now by throwing his good thoughts back in his face? And his sweet daughter, Rebekah, who has so often darned and patched my garments; who has always looked at me with such love and friendship, and never, God forbid, been wanton or spoken an unbecoming word like Borekh's daughter. Now must I say to her, 'I won't be your bridegroom; I can't'? But I really can't! And only you, dear God, know why."

Hershele felt embarrassed and ungrateful as Rebekah came back into the room with a decanter of brandy and pieces of honey cake.

He wished his worst enemy were before him, instead of this love-ly girl with her beautiful black eyes.

"One way or the other," said the rebbe, "this is God's busi-ness. We Jews must place ourselves in His care. Without His will, there's nothing. Let's take a drink—to your health!"

"To your health," Hershele answered, the only answer he could give to all the questions that now stood before him.

"But, have a drink, Hershele, don't be sad."

"I never drink, Rebbe."

"Are you afraid it will bother your bride? No, it's okay, don't worry; a little bit won't bother her—a little bit wakes the courage. Go ahead, take a little drink. We Jews don't drink to get drunk."

"But I have absolutely no love for whiskey."

"Love it for my sake," said the rebbe. "What's the significance of love, anyway? What do I know? People cry for love. People love what is their own. I never had love; nevertheless, now I love my wife, and I love my child more than life itself. You'll cry, you'll also love."

Hershele felt the rebbe had looked straight into his heart and actually understood why he couldn't consent to be Rebekah's bridegroom. That's why he had said, "One can cry for love."

"Do I love Mirele?" he asked himself. "Who knows when it comes to love? I know I can't live without her. One glance from her is enough to make me happy, so how can I darken my world by marrying another?"

"Drink," said the rebbe.

"I cannot."

"Do it for me," the rebbe asked again. Reluctantly, Hershele took a sip. The liquor was strong; tears formed in his eyes.

"Now I see you really can't drink liquor," said the rebbe. "You can't drink—and you can't answer the question I've asked you. And there's another thing you can't do: you can't counter what I've proposed."

The older man laid his hand on Hershele's shoulder. "Goodness, earlier I myself said one shouldn't say yes or no too quickly, especially about such important matters. Now I'm the one longing for a quick answer. I certainly don't expect you to respond right now. There's plenty of time. Deliberate as long as you like. If the answer turns out to be yes, you need only say you'll travel to Volozhin. I'll take it as a sign that I should not be seeking a different match for my Rebekah. It's all right, she'll wait for you. But if, God forbid, the reverse should be the case, let God be the witness between us both: I won't forsake you. And if I have so far loved you with an ulterior motive, I'll love you equally without one. You know the Gemara says: 'one envies his son and his pupil.'"

The rebbe spoke these last words with tears in his eyes. Rising from the table, he went over to embrace Hershele and kissed his head. Tears were also standing in Hershele's eyes. His heart was so softened by his rebbe's tenderness; he wanted to throw himself at his feet and confess his secret pain and wound. If only he could ask his rebbe's advice and seek his remedy—if such advice or remedy even existed—to heal him from his sickness and suffering. But how could one even talk of such things?

The head of the yeshiva sensed his grateful student's feelings and said, "Be peaceful, my son. Go home now. Through your tears I see the radiant light of your heart. God makes a pure heart; He created a pure heart in you that's worth more than anything else. Save your heart at all costs, Hershele. The heart is the door to the world beyond. My student, your heart is as clean as it was when the Creator gave it to you. Go home, remember my words, and if Borekh asks you, tell him to see me; I'll give him a clear answer, and you won't have to be afraid of him."

Leaving, Hershele caught another glimpse of Rebekah's big and radiant eyes. There was so much love in them, such moving pleas; his already torn heart was torn again.

"God created a pure heart in me," he told himself on his way back to the yeshiva. Then he cried out, "God, give me a clean heart, so that I will not be false to my good rebbe. Or better still, kill me before I become an ungrateful man to the good and faithful people I love."

Seven

Borekh did what he needed to do: he asked people great and small their opinion of Hershele, and everyone said he was getting a real kosher bargain. The only one he didn't ask was Hershele himself. He figured the question was unnecessary; hadn't Shlomo the matchmaker already said, "Why wouldn't he be pleased?"

"Is my daughter a cripple?" he asked himself. "Is she blind or unhealthy, God forbid? Can't she read and write just like the other girls? She'll be a great bride; a happiness for a man. She already knows more than her mother does.

"Not only that, he'll never worry about meager support from me. Meat, liver, tongue, and *kishke* won't be lacking, praise God. All Jewish children should be so lucky."

By the time he finished talking to himself, Borekh was convinced of Hershele's desire for Soreh-Feyge. He found himself becoming even more loving towards his daughter; he began buying her little gifts and giving her little kisses and hugs. He even began lecturing his sons, "I'll have joy from her; she'll light up my house and my world. 'This is Borekh's son-in-law,' people will say when they see him leading prayers before the congregation, or reading the Megillah at Purim, or studying in the yeshiva wearing a fine silver collar. And what will become of you, my dear sons? Just like your father, off to the slaughterhouse you'll go each morning, then off to the butcher shop where you'll spend the day arguing with the women. Oy, why can't you study and sing like him? Haven't I paid quite a few hard-earned rubles to your teachers? A downfall to you *schlimazels*."

Wherever he went, Borekh boasted of the match and invited people to witness the signing of his daughter's engagement contract, which, God willing, would take place after the holidays. Many girls envied the butcher's daughter and complained that Soreh-Feyge had come on to Hershele "the way a village *shikse* comes on to a prince." Several householders thought, "Hershele is too refined for Borekh's daughter and somebody should tell him so. But whose affair is it? Is it worth making Borekh an enemy by intervening in the match? If he's happy about it, we should be happy, too." Nevertheless, they begrudged Borekh his good fortune.

The yeshiva boys also resented the situation and constantly heckled Hershele. When he sold himself for a butcher's stomach, they suggested, he should also include a couple of fat cheeks for Borekh's daughter to slap after the wedding. But the insults didn't bother Hershele because he had a greater worry: that Mirele would hear the story before he could tell her it was all an error from start to finish.

But Mirele already knew; her own mother had broken the news to her. Since that evening during Purim when she'd seen Hershele on stage, a new feeling had been born in her. At first she believed she couldn't forget him because of his poverty and loneliness; that she only wanted to help him and provide for his health. Now, however, she longed for him. She wanted to see him, to speak with him, to sing with him. And even more—she felt a certain pain in her heart whenever she heard some girl going on and on about him, saying how she loved the fellow who played Joseph, and how she couldn't forget him for even two minutes. Mirele never admitted that she, too, loved him as much as that other girl—perhaps even more. She grew angry with herself and with him because she couldn't forget him.

On Wednesdays, when Hershele was supposed to come for a meal, she would leave to visit a friend so he wouldn't notice her agitation. Still, she felt her heart was crushing her the whole time she was gone. She longed to go home and see him—at least get a glimpse of him—that would be enough. But she denied her heart's longing and stayed out late, forgetting to eat, as if she were afraid of her own home.

As night fell, she went home, but she was so sad. She crept into a corner and began to cry, but when her mother found her and asked, "What's the matter, my child?" she didn't know what to say. She asked herself, "What's wrong with me? What's happening to me?"

The more she urged herself to stop thinking of him, the more she loved him. She thought of him at night when her protesting mind was asleep. Freed from her good sense, she saw him in her dreams like one of the heroes in her storybooks. She sang with him and listened to him read, and every word seemed so clever and lovable.

She also saw him as the always-poor yeshiva boy. His eyes begged her not to laugh at his poverty and desolation. Her heart went out to him; she wanted to cheer him up, and when she awoke, it was always with a heavy spirit.

"If only he would move away," she told herself. "I'd give him my last kopeck if he'd leave and become an influential, important man, the kind of man he wants to be. I'd send him money, write him letters—faithful loving letters. From afar I could tell him everything I'm feeling. I'd carry his letters close to my heart and read them ten times a day."

As the days passed, Brayndl became more and more concerned about her daughter. Her good and happy Mirele had become gloomy, picked at her food, spoke sadly, and always wanted to be alone. Yet Mirele answered all her mother's questions with "It's nothing, Mama. I'm fine, leave me alone."

One evening, looking at Mirele's sad expression, Brayndl tried to cheer her up by telling her the good news about Hershele. "I completely forgot," she began. "Perhaps this will please you. Last week, Borekh the butcher told me he's taking our yeshiva boy Hershele as a groom for his daughter Soreh-Feyge—taking him just as he is."

"What are you saying, Mama?" Mirele asked, turning pale.

"Just what I said. At the end of the holidays, Borekh intends to write the marriage agreement."

Mirele was silent, but her body trembled. "What's the matter, my daughter?" Brayndl said anxiously. "You're so pale."

"Mama, this can't be. He wouldn't do it."

"Why wouldn't he?" asked Brayndl. "Does Borekh come from such an exalted heritage that he can expect a more glorious match for his boorish daughter?"

"Not Borekh. Would Hershele want such a thing?" Mirele asked.

"Hershele?"

"Yes, Hershele."

"What are you talking about, Mirele? Is he a fool? Has he something better in the offing? Eating a meal here, a meal there; may God forgive me for pointing it out."

"But he's such a good scholar, Mama. He sings so beautifully. Can't he find a better match?"

"You've got a point, daughter; may God bless all parents with a son so learned and full of virtues. But don't forget, he's a pauper and alone in the world. What fine householder would take on a son-in-law without relatives to support him? What mother would find honor in having Shmuel the sentry as her in-law at the wedding?

"And this is not such a great honor for the daughter either. Though Borekh provided Hershele with a charitable meal each week, after the wedding, Berl the shoemaker can throw it in her face that he, too, fed her husband on his meager portion of bread.

"Let God not punish me for saying this, but who besides Borekh—who is himself merely a laborer who made good—would take him? He gets a diamond who's been wandering, poor thing, in the mud of poverty, and his daughter Soreh-Feyge gets the luck."

"But from whom did you hear this?" Mirele asked with a trembling voice.

"It's no secret. Borekh himself told me and practically invited me to the signing of the contract."

"And Hershele? Does he want it? Has Borekh asked him? Has he answered?"

"You're talking like a child," Brayndl replied sternly. "What do you mean, 'Does he want it'? Certainly Borekh asked and Hershele agreed."

"It's a lie, Mama. Borekh is just boasting. Hershele wouldn't do it."

Brayndl looked at her daughter in surprise. Mirele's cheeks were flushed and her excited heart shone through her eyes. "Why are you so worked up about this, my child?" she asked.

"Because nobody else worries about him, so I must. No, Mama, you can't let this happen."

"How is this my problem? Should I be getting into some-body else's business? Don't I have enough enemies already without ruining another person's marriage arrangements? Why is this up-setting you?"

"Don't you understand, this will bring him unhappiness. I'm going to tell him myself."

"What's come over you, my daughter? Listen to what you're saying. Are you his sister or his mother? A young woman can't just intervene in a match. Feh, you should be ashamed of yourself."

"The person who talked him into this is the one who should be ashamed," Mirele replied.

"Just tell me this: how can you feel so responsible for someone else? The boy eats a charitable meal at your mother's table once a week. There are plenty of householders to feed him without my meal. Perhaps things would be more comfortable for him else-where. Tell me, why don't the others worry about him? A town full of Jews—no evil eye—a rabbi, a head of the yeshiva, every-body says this is a good fortune for Hershele. But no, you have to be an unasked-for-redeemer trying to keep him from something he himself has already agreed to. Feh, you're speaking out of turn, my daughter."

"A town full of Jews, a rabbi, a head of the yeshiva," Mirele re-peated bitterly. "Do any of them know who Hershele is? Does the rabbi or the head of the yeshiva understand what he could be-come if luck led him into a fine home?"

"That's ridiculous, as I live and breathe," laughed Brayndl. "So now, perhaps, you know more than our rabbi? Suddenly, you're more of an expert on Hershele than his own rebbe, the head of the yeshiva? You know nothing! How in the world do you come to give this advice? People would laugh to the high heavens if they heard your pronouncements."

"Let them laugh, Mama. I won't let Hershele come to such unhappiness!"

"Don't shout at me, Mirele. The serving maid will hear and tell the rest of the town. Don't bring me more troubles, child. What's happened to your good sense?"

Mirele said nothing more. She angrily went to her room to sleep without supper.

Although she wondered what was wrong, it didn't occur to Brayndl to be suspicious of her daughter's behavior. She asked the maid if she knew why Mirele was so upset, if something unfortunate had happened during the day or if somebody had offended her.

The maid swore that, on the contrary, Mirele had stayed home all day and that nothing bad had happened. The previous night, Sheyndele the sewing-goods shopkeeper had visited and begged money from Mirele, probably as a charity gift.

"Oy, she'll ruin me," Brayndl said to herself. "Now I understand her anger: Sheyndele took money and didn't repay it. And because Mirele didn't want to tell me, she took her anger out on me and Borekh, as if it were our fault she lent money to Sheyndele. That must be it."

Before going to bed, Brayndl stopped at Mirele's door and asked softly, "At least tell me how much Sheyndele borrowed from you." When her daughter didn't answer, she assumed she was asleep and decided not to wake her.

But Mirele was awake. A thousand memories were running through her head. She was angry at herself, at her mother, at Hershele. She wanted to hate him, to ignore him completely in the future—but then she remembered how he looked at her the very first time they spoke, and when she asked him to take care of his health. And how lovingly his eyes had gazed at her from the stage.

"No, it can't be," she told herself. "How could he forget me? Maybe this is only Soreh-Feyge's boast? Yes, Soreh-Feyge boasted to her father, and Borekh believed her, and thinks Hershele is already hers."

Though she knew Soreh-Feyge well, Mirele now wanted to remember how she looked, to recall her in every detail to see if it were possible for Hershele to love her. At first when she closed her eyes she saw other girls whom she rarely ever thought about. But as hard as she tried, she struggled to conjure up Soreh-Feyge's face. What did her nose look like? What about her lips? She just remembered her as tall and wild. When at last Soreh-Feyge came into her mind's eye, Mirele had to admit she wasn't ugly; she even had a certain "girlish charm" about her. Young women pointed at her and said, "See how pretty she is?"

Suddenly Mirele jumped out of bed and walked barefoot to the table where she picked up a lamp and carried it to the mirror. She looked at her flaming cheeks, her shining eyes, and her long blond locks falling over her white neck. She gave herself an approving smile, confident she was as pretty as Borekh's daughter.

Having calmed herself, she crawled back into bed and vowed she would take the first opportunity to talk everything out with Hershele. She would not admit her own suffering on his account, but would find out what he really thought of her.

But when she finally fell asleep, she had a terrible dream. She found herself standing in the study house with the rabbi and the head of the yeshiva. She was fighting with them, but she didn't know why. Her mother was standing nearby, wringing her hands and crying, "Woe is me to hear such disgraceful words coming from a maiden." But this only made Mirele argue more forcefully.

Suddenly the rabbi turned into Shmuel the sentry with his big nightstick. Shmuel wanted to beat her, but as she escaped she found herself in the kitchen of Shifra, Berl the shoemaker's wife. Shifra was telling her serving maid, "You know, Mirele's groom took charity meals at my house."

The maid replied, "Ask Mirele if she'll give you back your pledge—the item you pawned."

As Shifra headed into the dining room, Mirele ran after her to return the pledge, but Hershele was lying on the bed overcome with charcoal fumes. His face was pale and his body thin. He reached out his hand to her and she ran to him, kissed him, and began to sob.

He took her into his arms and consoled her. "Soon I'll be one of the fine people, Mirele," he said and began to sing, "The sun and the moon and the eleven stars will bow to me." Suddenly he was standing on stage and she heard Soreh-Feyge's voice whispering in her ear, "See, Mirele, how handsome he is. I'll kiss him all over— over all his limbs."

All at once Borekh the butcher was standing behind her. "You vulgar girl," he shouted at Mirele. "You want to kiss a boy you're not related to? You can't do that!"

"I didn't say it," Mirele replied. "It was your daughter Soreh-Feyge!" But Borekh scowled and waved at Hershele to follow him.

As Hershele began to leave with Borekh, Mirele cried out, "No, Hershele, don't bring sorrow on yourself!" But Hershele never looked back. He just moved farther and farther away. Mirele's heart broke open and tears poured from her eyes. She cried freely until her mother, hearing her sobs, awakened her.

"My child," Brayndl said as she held Mirele's hand and quietly stroked away the terrifying dream.

"Mama," cried Mirele as she fell upon her mother's neck.

"It's all right, dear, you've had a bad dream," said Brayndl comforting her.

"Is it very late, Mama?" Mirele asked, pressing her mother's hand to her heart.

"No, child, it's still early," Brayndl answered. "I got up earlier than usual this morning. Today's a market day and I'm also going to visit your uncle's house. Tell me, dear, did Sheyndele ask you for more money? How much have you given her? It doesn't matter, we'll forgive the debt; it's probably destined."

"Sheyndele didn't ask for anything, Mama. On the contrary, she wanted to pay me back—with interest. But I never accept a percentage on charitable loans."

"Then what sorrow seized you last night? What has made you so upset?"

"It's nothing, Mama."

"Nothing, Mirele?"

"Please don't ask, Mama. Let it be. Oy, I'm so tired."

"All right, my child, the coffee isn't ready yet. You rest a little longer." Brayndl patted her daughter's hand and left the bedroom. Exhausted, Mirele fell back to sleep.

EIGHT

When Mirele awoke again, it was midmorning. "Where's my mother?" she asked the servant who was making the bed.

"Your mother left long ago. She told me to take care of you. 'She isn't healthy,' she said. What's the matter with you, Mirele?"

"I'm much better," Mirele replied. "Is today Wednesday?"

"It's Wednesday, exactly one week before Passover."

"Give me some water," Mirele asked as if in a hurry. "How late is it?"

"The clock just struck ten-thirty."

"Please get me some water."

By eleven o'clock Mirele was dressed. She knew Hershele would come for his meal between eleven and twelve, and the time dragged slowly as she waited for him. Minute by minute she hurried to the mirror, straightened her hair and the scarf around her neck, looked at herself in different poses and expressions, then went back to the window to see if he was coming down the street.

When she finally saw him from afar, her princess's pride suddenly vanished. The fantastic charm he possessed in her dream had disappeared, and he now looked, as usual, like a poor and beaten down schoolboy, meek and lifeless. She was embarrassed to have suffered so much over him. She quickly left the window, put on a warm jacket, and ran from the house. "I'm not giving in to my foolish heart," she told herself.

But as she headed out the door, she came face-to-face with him on the steps. Both stopped, their faces pale, and their hearts beating. She unwillingly glanced at him and saw his bright eyes; pity flooded her, and she began to feel bad about running from him.

Not wanting him to know she was turning back for his sake, Mirele said, "I completely forgot you were coming today. I have something to talk with you about. I'll be back soon." She then fled down the steps and hurried away without any idea of where she was going.

When she returned fifteen minutes later, she asked the serving maid, "Has he finished yet?" When the maid said, "He's still eating," Mirele waited in the kitchen. With a sly smile, the maid implied she knew what was going on, but unlike Mirele, she was enjoying herself.

Hershele, too, felt inner courage today. Once and for all, he had decided to tell Mirele how Borekh's boasting aggravated him— though he wouldn't tell her, God forbid, what was in his heart. "But she mustn't think I have no heart at all," he told himself. "And she should know, at least, that I understand why she's so angry with me. But I'm not guilty. God is my witness."

Mirele ran into her bedroom to take one final look in the mirror. She took a deep breath, patted her hair, and returned to the dining room. When Hershele saw her, his courage began to fade. Alone with her, he felt crazy and confused again; he forgot the speech he had prepared to explain his aggravation to her.

"How are you, Hershele?" she asked and sat down beside him.

"Thank you for asking," he answered, and her friendly look was enough to lift his sagging self-confidence.

"We haven't seen each other for a while," she said.

"Not since you spoke so kindly to me," he replied, "and gave me money to take care of my health."

"No, I saw you later than that—onstage when you played Joseph—didn't you see me there?" she asked, remembering every look he sent her from the stage.

"Of course, I saw you," he answered shyly. "You were sitting on the first bench next to your mother. Don't be offended that I didn't ask your permission before joining 'The Selling of Joseph.'"

"Why would I be offended? You weren't obliged to ask how I felt."

"Yes, I am obliged," he answered bravely. "You've been so faithful to me. Nobody else ever asks how I am; nobody else ever thinks of my health. But you ask and care. I don't know how I earned your kindness and friendship, but my heart feels you wish the best for me."

"Your heart is not lying," Mirele said.

"I believe it more now that I hear it from your lips," he answered with a smile. "And that's why you'd be entitled to take offense that I didn't ask your permission before agreeing to be in the play."

"If I didn't want you to act and sing, I wouldn't have come to hear you. That's the proof. If I hadn't come, I'd never have known what you can do. Now I believe you can become a greater man, if only you believe in your own abilities. But what good are my words? I fear you love something else which will keep you from being happy."

"Who doesn't want to be happy?" Hershele asked.

"You don't want to be happy!" she erupted angrily.

"What are you saying?" he replied. "Perhaps you think what people are saying is true? Such talk is of no consequence; it's awful gossip. I'm poor and alone. I can't shut Borekh's mouth; he can say whatever he pleases. But I can tell you he is completely wrong. He hasn't asked me. And while he doesn't ask, I must remain silent. He is a householder to whom I'm beholden."

"I see," said Mirele. "I believe you; let's not speak any more about it. Rather, tell me, Hershele, why are you always so pale?"

"I didn't know I was pale," he answered. "I'm healthy, thank God."

"Don't you believe me? Come to the mirror and see for yourself."

Before he had time to say a word, she kindly took his hand, and led him to the mirror. He was confused and embarrassed. When he looked in the mirror, he only saw Mirele: her cheeks shone like a pair of lovely roses, and in her eyes a radiant fire burned. Suddenly he saw himself as well—and was frightened by his pallor.

The copper bowl in the study house that served him as a mirror hadn't revealed his ghostly complexion. Now, however, he saw his reflection clearly and wondered how a person could be so pale. A heavy sigh tore from his heart.

Mirele understood his shock, and not releasing his hand, scolded him, "You see, you haven't obeyed me and taken care of your health as you promised."

Confused, Hershele almost forgot he was standing hand in hand with Mirele, the one he would give his soul for. When she began to speak, he felt as if he were awakening from a dream. He didn't just see her in the mirror, he sensed her standing next to him. "Mirele," he whispered and gave her hand a heartfelt squeeze. Wondering where he found the courage to say her name and squeeze her hand, he dropped his eyes in embarrassment. Mirele looked into the mirror and saw a sudden reddening of his pale cheeks.

Mirele led Hershele back to the table and sat down beside him. "You see," she said, "I told you the truth. You're not well. You're suffering; you're longing for something, but you don't say what. At least you know I'm your friend, and your health is very important to me."

"I'm healthy, believe me," he said, as if pleading with her. "Perhaps my heart is sick inside me. Yes, my heart often hurts, but there's no remedy for it."

"What hurts your heart? Tell me," she asked.

"Can one explain the heart?" he answered.

"To a true friend, a faithful friend, one can explain even the heart. Are you still not sure I'm such a friend to you?"

"But if I tell you, you'll become angry. You won't want to be my friend any longer—even though I'm not guilty, and God himself is my witness."

"Be sure, I will not hold you accountable if you're not guilty."

But Hershele remained silent. Either he didn't have the courage or he didn't have the words to express his heart's pain. Mirele watched him intently, and felt what was in his heart. After a few quiet moments, she asked with a sweet smile, "You don't believe I won't be angry?"

"If you say it's true, I must believe you," he replied in a trembling voice. "Otherwise, I would never let these words out of my mouth. Mirele, my heart longs for you. I myself don't know how it began, but for at least a year, I haven't been able to forget you. What I think, I think for you. What I do, I do for your sake. Though it's a sin before God, I won't lie. For the entire year, I've been studying Gemara day and night for you, so that one day I would be respectable enough to speak with you. I prayed, I fasted, I petitioned God to make me rich just so I could provide for you. I don't want you to ever lack for anything good in this world.

Mirele, everything I've been doing, I've been doing for you. So now, go ahead and be angry with me. But remember this: you yourself said my heart doesn't lie. This is what my heart is saying, and it is telling the truth."

Mirele dropped her eyes. She heard Hershele's ardent words—even more impassioned than when he'd spoken onstage before Mother Rachel's tomb. Then she couldn't take her eyes off him; now she was feeling shy and could no longer look at him, although his words were even sweeter and more beloved than before.

In vain he waited for her answer. She sat silently, not taking her eyes off the floor. "You're angry and you have a right to be," he began, pain in his voice. "I'm sinning before God—and before you. God knows I'm not to blame, may He forgive me, but how can you know? And I don't want you to forgive me, Mirele. Just say you don't want to see me any more and I'll leave; I'll move away. I'll obey you in everything. And wherever I go, I'll pray to God for your happiness, Mirele, not for my own. I'll study day and night for you, learn Torah and the wisdom of the sages, until one day I can join the respectable people. Perhaps then you will forgive me."

When she finally looked up, she saw tears in his eyes. And with tears in her own beautiful eyes, she smiled at him lovingly. "My friend, my dear friend," she said quietly.

"Mirele."

"Hershele."

And neither of them remembered whose faithful arms secretly brought them together and pressed their burning lips into their first innocent and loving kiss.

NINE

Only a few hours earlier when Hershele had arrived at Mirele's mother's house, he looked poor, alone, timid, and lifeless. When he left, he looked heartened and happy. And just as Mirele had earlier been embarrassed by the turmoil this poor schoolboy had caused in her life, she now felt joyful and proud to have brought the war in her heart to a dear, sweet peace.

"He's so different from how he seemed earlier," she thought, as she sat by the window watching him go. "It's as if a weight has been lifted from his shoulders. He carries his head high; his step is sure, and he stands tall and proud. If only his clothes weren't so ragged. If only his home weren't the shabby old study house where he's so alone, where he lives among such inferior boys, and where no one understands him."

Slowly a plan began to form in her mind. The next time her mother was away at the marketplace or out fabric shopping for their holiday dresses, she'd write a letter to Hershele that would ostensibly arrive from a rich uncle. In the envelope she would include money for the purchase of new clothes. Hershele would show the letter to Mirele's mother so she wouldn't ask how he'd suddenly acquired such a fortune.

As Mirele went to her writing table, a thousand thoughts began to rush through her head. "What tone would an uncle use in such a letter?" she asked herself. "Would it be better for an aunt to write and not the uncle himself?"

Mirele returned to the window and saw Hershele exuding the same fantastic charm she'd dreamt about, only now the fear and darkness were gone. Light was shining all around her, and her heart was full of happiness and hope.

And the same was true for Hershele. As he walked, the sun shone brightly. The snow and ice were gone; the streets were dry, and the air was fresh and warm. He couldn't remember seeing the world so free and beautiful. The old sad and downtrodden way he'd trudged to Brayndl's house had disappeared.

Everything in the town seemed new—new streets and new houses—and he wondered why he was suddenly seeing everything for the first time. How pretty the apothecary shop looked with its large half-round window. He stopped to marvel at the big crystal jar on display. It was filled with colored waters, and he looked to see if the flask was made of red, blue, and green glass, or if the waters within were coloring it. A little further along he stopped at Noyekh the watchmaker's window to admire all the different clocks and timepieces.

He continued on, not even noticing his path, until he found himself outside the town. A broad field, only now free of snow, stretched before his eyes. A little stream of clear water rushed along, the sun reflecting on its surface; and on the horizon at the edge of the heavens, he saw a quiet, secret forest.

"Oh, how wonderful it must be there," he thought as he crossed the field to the woods, and his heart sang freely before God and the silent trees. He didn't want to rest and moved quickly, not even feeling the ground beneath his feet. With every breath, he felt renewed strength and warm blood coursing through his body. He jumped, ran, and wandered, not noticing the time, until the sun began to set and a cold breeze chilled him. It was time to go back to the yeshiva.

When he entered the study house, long past evening prayers, he was surprised at how sad and dark it seemed. On long winter nights when all the schoolboys huddled around the long tables with their open Gemaras and endeavored to out sing and shout each other, bright candles burned on every table and bookstand, and the warmth of the oven was felt at the doorway. On such nights the study house seemed a radiant, warm, clean palace. He used to go to his bookstand near the Holy Ark with pleasure. He truly wanted to learn; and when he sang the words, studying was a true concert from which he drew strength.

But now it was the break for *Pesach,* and the study house was silent, like a railway station when the train is gone. Somewhere in a corner he saw a lamp burning. Perhaps, he thought, a student was studying a Talmudic passage about Passover, in case the provider of his charity meal asked a question about *chametz* or some other detail related to *Pesach.* In another corner, stood another boy in front of a bookstand. On his knee he balanced a book of commentary, and was so deep in thought, he didn't notice the candle wax melting and running over his fingers.

Why had he returned, Hershele asked himself? Didn't he know the details of the Passover passage? Couldn't he answer, "How was the Wicked Child's question worse than the Wise Child's?" He didn't care about it anymore; he should be sleeping, resting. Hadn't he studied and slaved day and night over the long winter, just in case this little passage would please the householder who invited him for seder, or bring a little pleasure to his wife, though she wouldn't understand a single word of what he was saying?

Perhaps his knowledge of Torah would also be worthy in the eyes of the householder's daughter, as pleasing as a new garment, hat, or neckerchief in honor of the holiday—all of which he lacked. If she dressed up in her expensive gown and jewelry to please him, then his clever knowledge of holy Torah and hair-splitting arguments must be his fine clothes, his jewelry, his charm.

In another room, a circle of boys sat together with their needles and threads, stitching up holes and mending their poor and tattered clothes. They told each other stories they'd heard or read, and looked happy, as if they lacked for nothing. Hershele watched them, and in the blink of an eye, a sudden chill came over him. He stood by the *bimah*, his head drooping, and a strong feeling grabbed his heart.

"How have I come to this?" he asked himself. "Is this my home? Must I live here forever? No, Mirele's right. She tells me to travel far away to study and learn. Why not? If only I could go right now. If only it weren't just before Passover. The sooner I go, the sooner I'll come back to her. Oy, how can I live through these next few days?"

Something drew him back outside. He wanted to run away to a place where he could make a name for himself. The study house was now too confining for his overflowing heart, and he sought a broader world. He stood on the steps and saw the moon shining in the clear blue sky. She, too, seemed to look at him, her gaze friendly and loving.

He remembered learning in school that she was once as large and radiant as the sun. It irked him now that she'd been foolish enough to get mixed up in the creation of the world and that the Creator had struck her and reduced her size. She seemed to him still sad about her sin, and Hershele prayed to God to release her from her flaw.

A quiet breeze blew across his face, throwing his hair over his forehead. It blew into his heart as well, and the cold made him shiver. He ran back into the study house, went to his bookstand, and lit a candle. He wanted to sit and study, but instead of a portion of the Talmud, a Psalm came into his mind, and he began to sing, "He raises up the poor out of the dust," in a voice that was fresher and lighter than any time before.

The other schoolboys quickly closed their books and put away their needles. They ran to hear the unexpected concert. Hershele, standing on the *bimah,* sang for half an hour. The feelings had finally found a way to express themselves through his voice, pouring out in sweet trills like a clear brook from a deep spring. A prayer to God the Almighty and All-knowing; a deeply emotional prayer without words arising to heaven from the yeshiva.

The boys stood in awe, each holding his breath so as not to interrupt. They'd never heard him sing like this; and when he stopped, one of his friends said, "Hershele, it's a real pity to sell this gift that God has given you. And to whom? To Borekh the butcher for his daughter, who won't expand your mind as a nice woman would, a beautiful woman, which, as the Talmud says, is one of the three things that increases a man's self-esteem."

"What a voice you have," called out another. "One couldn't buy such a heavenly gift for ten thousand rubles."

"You may be angry at me for saying so, Hershele, but I tell you again," said a third, "if Brayndl, who gives you a charity meal on Wednesdays, would take you as the bridegroom for her only daughter, I would counsel you to accept. That is a girl who would increase a man's self-esteem!"

"That Brayndl is a typical woman," interrupted a fourth. "Does a woman understand the worth of such a voice? But I know Mirele; she has a feeling for such things. She's the best in the city. I'm amazed she isn't already in love with you! Why not sing for her, Hershele? When she hears you sing, I tell you—"

"If you ask me, this is what you should do," said a boy who'd been standing for a while near a bookstand. He was the boy from Vilna, who had a wealth of worldly knowledge and a bit of a singing voice himself. He had played Judah in "The Selling of Joseph." It was said the Vilner had studied with a disciple of Moses Mendelssohn, and he was known to have a great mind; therefore, everyone now stood still, straining to hear his opinion.

"If you ask me," the Vilner began, "don't listen to them, Hershele. Scrape together a few rubles for expenses and head to Altunien or Zulthern where there is a fine chorus. Show them your voice, sing for them, they'll see what a throat you have. Once they hear your voice, they'll grab you with both hands. I tell you, your voice is a very rare and fine tenor. You also have such fine feeling in your singing and a good ear. You could become one of the best in the world and give the greatest concerts before kings and princes, do you understand?"

"But what will become of his Torah?" asked the Slutsker. "Will he throw away the Gemara, stop studying, and become a libertine?"

"You ass!" the Vilner answered in exasperation. "Who is calling for him to throw away Torah? I only mean he can attain a higher level through his beautiful voice. Hershele, the world needs Torah wisdom and music, too! As it says in the Talmud, 'It is not possible to have one without the other. One must have a craft as well as Torah. Happy is he whose vocation is the making of perfume; woe to him who makes leather.'

"And if Bezalel ben Uri and Oholiab son of Ahisamach had studied Torah as much as Moses and Joshua, who would have built the Tabernacle and made the Ark with all its vessels? Only a fool who hasn't studied even the Pirkei Avot can believe all Jews, big and small, rich and poor, must be occupied in studying Torah day and night. Torah can only exist if she is studied in concert with a profession. As the Gemara says, 'Every Torah that doesn't have a profession with it will be erased at its end.'"

"But singing is no profession!" the Slutsker countered.

"Singing is a wisdom," replied the Vilner. "There need to be rabbis in the world, teachers, tradespeople, and wise men also. Everyone should study and master that which moves him, that to which he is most suited."

"Why don't *you* learn to sing?" Hershele asked the Vilner.

"Hey, brother, if I had your voice, I'd already be famous! But what's the use? Singing is something you're born with, a gift from God, and you will be judged if you don't take such a fabulous voice and become like the Vilner Balebesl, who amazed the world with his throat, his voice, and his fiddle!"

Thus began a conversation about the Vilner Balebesl. Each told the legends he'd heard in his own town. One said the Balebesl had once prayed in a very large city—Paris, Istanbul, or Alexandria—and a grand prince, a strange millionaire, came from a great distance to hear him and purchased the Balebesl's throat—after his death, of course—for a hundred thousand dinars in gold.

"What use would he have for the Balebesl's dead throat?" someone asked. "Can a dead throat sing?"

"You're an idiot," said the boy. "Go ask the prince your questions! I'm just telling you what I heard. You ask what use is a dead throat? I guess he had some reason for wanting it."

"You've never been a grand prince," remarked another. "The throat of a famous singer is worth as much as a diamond. Why do you think people pay so much for diamonds? A diamond, per se, is no more than a pebble—a pretty pebble, of course—but what does one have when one owns such a pebble? It's just that it's a rare thing. The dead throat of a famous singer, naturally, is also a rare thing. That's why a grand prince would desire such a treasure and think it worth millions. While to us it isn't worth a kopeck."

Another legend was told that when the Balebesl was a baby still lying in his cradle, the world already rang with the sound of his sweet little voice. Cantors traveled to Vilna from miles away to hear him. His mother would pluck him out of the cradle, and the cantors would stick him with pins so he'd begin to cry, and they could hear his sweet voice.

Still others recounted more legends, and there was no end to the questions and answers that followed. Finally, the Vilner boy, who'd been listening the whole time and smiling to himself, suddenly banged on his reading stand and shouted, "Who's telling stories about the Vilner Balebesl? You monkeys! Vilna is my hometown. Ask me, I'll tell you!"

"I want to hear," Hershele said. "Tell us."

"Then you all must listen," said the Vilner, "and not interrupt while I'm talking!"

"Good," they all agreed.

"But before I begin to tell you about the Balebesl, I need to give you a brief introduction to Vilna itself. Do you know how many famous people come from my birthplace Vilna? Where else will you find such learned rabbinical scholars as reside in Vilna? Where else will you find such schools and study houses as we have in Vilna? In what other city will you find so many charitable organizations? Or benevolent societies; there are so many, I can't even name them all. No city in the world has as many as my Vilna! And it's not for nothing she's called 'The Jerusalem of Lithuania.' Just as Jerusalem was then, so is our Vilna now. No other city has given so many sages and holy books—sages like Reb Mordechai Aaron Gintsburg, like Adam Hakohen Lebenzon, his son Mikah

Joseph, Reb Yudl Shereshevski, Reb Matityahu Strashun, Reb Mordechai Plungian, Reb Shmuel Yosef Finn, and Reb Kalman Schulman. Perhaps you don't know who they were, but you would if you read and knew what was going on in the world.

"You should know that all these wise men were our crowns; they made our losses whole again, brought back our beautiful holy language, and people reading their books 'lick their fingers' from the sweetness. Oy, Hershele, if you were to read their books written in the holy language, your eyes would be opened."

"Aren't you special!" the Slutsker blurted out. "Hershele, he told you to travel abroad to become a choir master. Now he tells you to study the devil's books! Don't listen to him. Vilna is given over to heretics, and he urges you to become a heretic as well, like the rebellious Jeroboam, the son of Nabat. He is a sinner and causes others to sin!"

"By praising something you end up condemning it," Hershele said to the Vilner.

"You Slutsker bum!" the Vilner shouted. "You think your precious Slutsk is a city? It's a village full of peasants, and you're the worst of the lot!"

A great argument broke out between Vilna and Slutsk until Hershele sang out in a Gemara-tune: "'You began speaking of a pitcher and ended up talking about barrels.' Stop already! You started to tell us about the Balebesl, and now you're ranting about your proud Vilna. Everyone knows about Vilna's famous citizens; are you saying anything new? Why don't you just go on and tell us properly who the Balebesl was and what happened to him, and don't mix in extraneous matters."

"It's human nature to recount all the advantages of one's birthplace when asked to tell about a particular person," the Vilner answered. "Again, as I said at the beginning, I wished to present a brief introduction."

"But your introduction has gone on long enough," said Hershele. "Now tell us, we want to hear the story of the Balebesl."

"Good! This is what I heard in my Vilna," the Vilner began. "He was already famous as a small child. One could hear a great voice, a holy vessel in the making.

"About his singing there's nothing more to be said. Everyone knows there's never been another like him among the Jews. As for his fiddle playing—no one would disagree: he hasn't been surpassed since the time of King David. We have old people who remember him still and swear they heard words spoken by his fiddle when he played it. People say he had 'David's harp' in his instrument. To this very day it's said the Balebesl's fiddle didn't just play—it talked. It spoke to the heart and brought tears to the eyes of everyone who heard him. He brought such feeling from the strings!

"He was also astonishingly handsome, studied skillfully, and was very pious—as they were in those days. Perhaps if he were with us now, he'd be a great *maskil*. So, of course, many offers were made; he was engaged to the only daughter of a very wealthy man when he was only a child. The wedding took place at his bar mitzvah and immediately thereafter he was made choirmaster in the Great Vilna Synagogue.

"You should know what an honor this was. In the Great Vilna Synagogue the cantor was always an old and experienced man. Nevertheless, the Balebesl was selected while still a boy. That alone shows how exceptional he had become in his singing. They called him 'Balebesl' because it shouldn't be said that the cantor of the Great Vilna Synagogue was just a lad. So they used the term for a young married man.

"In years and in height, however, he was still a child, and in order to be heard he had to stand on a bench. If you heard him praying even once, you'd never forget it. His Jewish melodies, his Jewish emotion—even a heart literally made of stone would soften and tears would flow. Once the word got out, people came from all corners of the earth to hear him.

"He received invitations from the greatest congregations to come and pray with them. But Vilna wouldn't permit him to go. Then one day, the demons of evil brought a powerful and wealthy man from the great city of Warsaw. He managed to talk the Vilna community into letting the Balebesl travel to Warsaw. He was to pray and then come straight home.

"So the Balebesl prayed in Warsaw and he took Warsaw by storm! Princes, dukes, and duchesses came to hear him. And that was his undoing. Being so honored, he forgot who and what he was, and he was taken unaware when a greater temptation came upon him: he let himself be convinced to give a concert in the great Warsaw theater.

"Such a concert had never been heard before. One young *Fräulein,* the daughter of a great Count—she herself could sing and was a great beauty—fell so in love with him at the concert that her doctors were in despair of her life if she didn't marry him.

"Understand, it took plenty of money and effort to convince the Balebesl to go to her. He didn't know what was going on. He simply thought: she wants to hear me sing and play the violin, why not? Particularly as she was a connoisseur and was also a singer, he thought to hear her sing as well.

"But 'the voice of woman is a temptation,' says the Gemara, and this was the first stumbling block. He sang a wonderful private concert for her which left him exhausted and sweating heavily with emotion. He went into another room to rest, but the girl, who had been waiting for this moment, followed him. She took out an expensive silken scarf—said to be enchanted—and wiped the sweat from his face. Then she cooled him with an expensive fan, also full of sorcery, and blew on him until he forgot the world and himself. His heart began to burn with a terrible love for the *Fräulein*. He felt he would die for her. From that day on, they say, he fell into an ever-deepening melancholy. He stopped singing; he stopped eating, and he even stopped talking. Nobody knew what was the matter.

"There was no one he could pour his heart out to, and he couldn't explain how he longed and burned with love for her. He still had enough strength to resist the Evil Inclination, but the enchantment wouldn't let him leave Warsaw. He kept postponing his trip back home—for another day, another week—until his wife and the Vilna community couldn't wait any longer and came running to Warsaw.

"You can imagine their horror and sadness upon finding their beloved jewel so sad, so darkened. His wife fell on his neck with bitter tears. 'What's the matter, my heart, my life?' she pleaded, revealing her great love for him. 'What do you need, our dear cantor?' asked the great people of Vilna. They wrung their hands and tears flowed as they looked at his pale face.

"But no use; he spoke no words. He looked at his wife with compassionate eyes; his heart went out to her as she sobbed and cried. He knew she was faithful to him, that she would give her life for him, but how could that help him now? His heart had suddenly become unbound from her and had, through heavy witchcraft, become bound to that *Fräulein* for whom he longed and pined.

"He looked at the tears of the fine people of Vilna, people who'd always extended their hands to him, honored him, made sure he lacked for nothing—but he couldn't show them the wound in his heart. His pain became even greater. He prayed to God for a quick death; the world was ugly to him. The *Fräulein* was now life itself to him; yet he couldn't even hope to have her.

"The greatest doctors and professors were brought to him. They couldn't ascertain the nature of his illness. They only said he yearned too strongly for something, and his heart was breaking from it.

"Only he knew what the problem was. Should he divorce his wife? Why? What had she done to him? How would she survive it? How could he be so evil-hearted? And if he did have the heart to divorce her, what would come of it? The *Fräulein* wasn't Jewish, of course. Would he change his faith? It would be no small thing to speak about this, or even to think about it.

"He had a truly Jewish heart—everyone knew it as soon as they heard the Jewish sob in his sweet sad melodies. No, he had no alternative than to hold his sorrow in his heart and suffer quietly—longing until bit by bit he was extinguished like a candle, waiting for death to free him.

"And that's just how it was: he was taken back to Vilna. He didn't want to pray at the cantor's desk, he couldn't. He didn't talk to anybody. He hung his violin on the wall as the Levites once had by the rivers of Babylon. How could he continue singing Jewish songs when his heart was bound to a *Fräulein*, the Countess who'd worked a spell on him!

"But on those rare occasions when the urge came upon him—while leaving home or standing in a corner of the study house with his prayer shawl let down and his face dreamy and pale as chalk—he would suddenly sing a quiet passage that would move a stone.

One could hear within it how his pure soul prayed to God to be released from his suffering and bewitched body.

"Baths were prepared for him using expensive wines and cold water, but all was in vain; nothing helped. One day, sitting in an ice-cold bath, he suddenly began to sing the penitential prayer for sick children. Everyone nearby wept; they could clearly see how he poured his whole heart into the tune. His eyes were suddenly radiant; his face began to shine again as it once had. The enchantment gave way—but his body had no more strength for living. Immediately after he was helped out of the bath, he said his confession, said goodbye to his good friends and acquaintances, asked his wife's forgiveness, and quietly died like a holy man. He died young, poor thing, after long, hard suffering and distress. Nobody had any idea how much."

Hershele's heart began to choke with compassion; tears formed in his eyes. "I'm angry at your Vilners!" he said. "Why did they let him go to Warsaw? If they hadn't, perhaps he would still be alive today and would not have suffered so much."

"If only people at the time had known who and what the Balebesl was," said the Vilner. "But this was a story from Satan. They let him go, yes; but the beloved songbird tore himself from the gilded cage, a cat grabbed him and tore him to pieces. And we may never know such a cantor again. Unless you, Hershele, choose to become one. You have the voice, the throat, and the feeling for it; all you're lacking is luck. A Jewish lad must find his own way to go from small to big. Just take care, Hershele, about love! Always remember that you're a Jew, and don't cast your eye on the countesses and *fräuleins* who'll come to hear you. I'm very afraid for you. Women could fall in love with you when you sing. It could happen now while you're poor, and even more so when you're performing concerts and become rich."

The night after this conversation, Hershele couldn't sleep. The Balebesl's face was never out of his imagination. He saw him standing, white as chalk, his head bowed in deep contemplation. His prayer shawl fell from his shoulders and slipped to the ground; quietly and sadly a sweet, deep, moving melody poured out as the desolate soul prayed to be parted from his tortured body. Hershele wanted to fall on the Balebesl's neck and console him, say he understood his wound, and felt his suffering. He wanted to help him with his whole heart, or at least ask consolation from him, so they could cry together over their mutual pain and inner suffering.

"And who better than I to know how terrible were his sorrows?" Hershele thought. "Didn't I pray for death when I had no hope that Mirele could become my friend? And Mirele didn't work sorcery on me; Jews don't do that. And why would she have to? My heart is drawn to her like a magnet.

"It's possible there was also no enchantment in the Balebesl's case, but rather a feeling, a pull. The difference is that, first, he wasn't drawn to a Jewish daughter, and second, he already had a loving wife. But why should I be afraid? Would Mirele part from me? Or would I exchange her for even the richest and most beautiful countess in the world? Never! I won't allow such a temptation to overtake me. But I have to find a way to become as respectable as the Balebesl. Whether it's from singing, or by scholarship, I must become respectable—for her, for Mirele!"

Then he remembered how his friend from Vilna recommended certain books owned by his town's respectable people and sages that, he said, would open his eyes. He wondered what could be in such books. How could one get to see them, read them, and perhaps even study from them? He decided to talk this over with the Vilner on the following day to find out how one becomes a critical thinker. He knew he had to achieve this status; Mirele had to know he wasn't just a yeshiva boy who could do nothing more than study holy books and sing.

His plans, hopes, and dreams began to weave together in his head and pulled him into the future. He imagined himself performing concerts with Mirele beside him. He didn't even look at anyone else; Mirele was the most beautiful, the cleverest, and the richest of them all. He was rich, too, and had done well by all his friends. He had made the Vilner rich, and even let the Slutsker attend one of his concerts in Warsaw's Grand Theater without a ticket. He gave lots of money to the head of the yeshiva, built him a fine house, bought him many expensive books, and found a very respectable bridegroom for his daughter Rebekah. He provided her with a large dowry, and Mirele loved her too, like a sister. He didn't even forget Borekh the butcher and made him rich—rich as Korach. But he wouldn't look at Soreh-Feyge—it seemed Mirele hated her and refused to have her in her sight.

Hershele also remembered his poor mother, lying so young in the graveyard of their tiny town. He wanted to build her a big tombstone with gold letters on it. Having never known his father, he decided to seek out his two poor sisters to learn where he was buried. His heart ached as he recalled how poor his two sisters were when last he saw them. Now more than ever before he wanted to become rich and important. He imagined he would go to see them, but they wouldn't recognize him. He would tell them he had a greeting from their brother Hershele who was taken away as an orphan. They'd be so happy with the gifts he'd apparently sent, and would ask, "How is he doing, where is he now?"

That's when he'd tell them the truth—just like Joseph told his brothers—"I am your brother Hershele!" And they'd throw themselves on his neck and cry out in happiness.

"Don't thank me, don't kiss me," he'd answer. "Thank Mirele, kiss Mirele! She made me a respectable man. She gave me the strength and the will to rise in status. If it weren't for her, I would forever have remained a poor dejected yeshiva boy living in a study house. I'd be as poor as you. But now I'm rich and want to make you rich, too."

They would fall on Mirele's neck and thank her and kiss her. Their poverty wouldn't embarrass her. "They're beautiful," she'd say. "They can sing, too, and from this moment on, they'll be rich as well."

With such sweet thoughts he fell asleep as dawn came.

TEN

Mirele hurried to carry out her plan to clothe Hershele using her own money and without her mother knowing about it. As soon as she left the window where she'd so happily and lovingly watched Hershele head down the street, she began to compose a letter, supposedly from Hershele's rich uncle, that would also include money for new clothes.

But as she wrote the letter, she felt she lacked the appropriate Hebrew phrases that a man—the head of a household—would use, and that her tone was too weak and womanly. So she tore up the letter and began again, this time writing as if she were Hershele's aunt. This letter turned out much better. Happy and proud of herself, she waited impatiently for her mother's return so she could read it aloud to her.

Brayndl came home hungry and even before throwing off her coat shouted to Deborah the serving maid, "Prepare the table, I'm fainting from hunger!"

"Mama, it's good you're finally home," Mirele said happily as she helped her mother take off her fur coat. "I, too, have hardly had a bite to eat all day. Quickly, Deborah, please give us some food!"

"I can't even leave the house," Brayndl said with a reproachful tone. "What a child! If I don't bring the food and stand over her, she completely forgets to eat. Woe is me! Of course you're feeling faint!"

Mirele was truly hungry and ate heartily, which greatly pleased her mother—who'd never seen such an appetite in her elegant daughter. Mirele now seemed more beautiful and mature than ever; her cheeks were flushed with healthy color, and her eyes shone with radiant fire. Even her lovely sweet lips were redder now; and when Mirele rose from her seat, Brayndl thought she looked taller and slimmer. An unfamiliar sweet feeling came over her as she looked at her beloved child. Unable to restrain herself, she rushed to Mirele and happily hugged and kissed her. She then quietly warded off the evil eye.

Mirele tenderly hugged her mother in return. "Listen, Mama, Hershele was here today. He waited for you. He received some sort of letter from an uncle and aunt; they sent him money for new clothes. He asked if you'd help him; if you'd go to the tailor's and buy him something suitable to wear. I hope I did the right thing, keeping the letter and the money here. In the study house, God forbid, it might be taken away."

"How much money?" Brayndl asked.

"I don't know; perhaps twenty-five or thirty rubles. Here, I have the letter; I haven't counted the money. He asked me to read it over, but I've had no time. I said I'd read it to you."

"One has to count money," Brayndl instructed her daughter. "Hershele would never accuse you of anything, but it's important to know how much is there. Show me the letter."

Mirele took out an envelope that was smudged and dirty and handed it to her mother. Brayndl immediately took out the money and counted it. "Thirty-five rubles," she said, marveling at the amount. "Lucky fellow! He must be shouting in celebration. Now, of course, he won't have to consider Borekh's marriage offer."

"No, Mama, you're wrong; he's the same as always. I mean, the money won't change him. He said, now that they've found him, his rich uncle and relatives wouldn't forget him, and any time he asked they'd send him more."

Brayndl said in wonder, "So that's how it is? You can know someone for a hundred years and not really know who he is! I had no idea he had such rich aunts and uncles; who knew he had no need to suffer? Yet he's always pleased me, like a silken, elegant boy. People always thought he must come from fine stock. Read the letter, daughter."

"To my beloved, dear nephew, Hershele love," Mirele began, pretending to have a bit of difficulty with the unfamiliar hand-writing. "I must first report, dear nephew, that your uncle and I and our dear children are all well—may God hear the same from you—and may we quickly see you safely home, amen!

"Second, I report that as soon as my husband, your dear uncle, received your letter—hearing that you're alone there, poor thing, without a ruble in your pocket for expenses, shoes, and clothes—he, your uncle, wanted to rescue you and bring you home. 'Enough already with the wandering far from home!' he said, and we all replied he should go fetch you; you've studied long enough. How long should one put off one's life for the sake of learning?

"It's sad here without you! When you were here, our house was full of song and happiness. Since you departed, we long for your re-turn. Everyone always asks, 'Where is our dear good Hershele? What is he doing now? Does he still sing so sweetly? Who listens to him? God knows if his listeners understand the precious gift the Master of the Universe has given us in his sweet voice!'

"No hour or day goes by that one of us doesn't recall you with love and faithfulness. That's why your uncle wanted to immediately travel and bring you home. But it's almost Passover, and you know what a busy time this is. For now, he sends thirty-five rubles for clothes. But be sure they are well made: not too long, not like a yeshiva boy's. They should be suitable for wearing when you soon, God willing, come home to us.

"What more should I tell you? Everything is, praise God, the same with us here. Thanks be to He who lives forever for our health and livelihood!

"Your uncle will probably write separately; he's out now about his business. But I'm in a hurry to send this letter so you have time to engage a good tailor and be well dressed for Passover. Have your clothes made well and fashionably. You weren't born, God forbid, wearing a yeshiva boy's clothing—and you shouldn't be a yeshiva boy much longer.

"Give a friendly greeting in your uncle's name and in my name to the good dear householders who've been taking care of you, whose bread you eat. In particular, we thank God, blessed be He, for the wealthy widow Mistress Brayndl, may she live and be healthy. Since you wrote us that you've found favor in her eyes and that she treats you like family, we can't forget her dear beloved name. We pray to God, blessed be He, for her and her dear household, that He always brightens their way. May their mitzvah and kindness be remembered in heaven and in God's book, where all good stories are written.

"Show her this letter, my nephew, so she knows her kindness is appreciated and that you were not, God forbid, born under a stone. Praise God—with your fine family background you have no reason to be ashamed of your uncles and aunts. Don't worry that you've been a yeshiva boy far from home for so long, studying the holy Torah. Don't worry; we'll yet receive great happiness from you, and you'll remember these times happily for many years.

"All our children send greetings, Hershele. The boys are in *cheder* now, the girls are getting ready to go dancing at the wedding of your previous rabbi's daughter. I'll also be attending the wedding; but as Passover is almost upon us, I'll only stay for the bride's veiling ceremony. I've bought a fine wedding gift for presentation after the groom's speech; I'll have them proclaim, 'This is given by the splendid hero Hershele, a student of the bride's father!'

"If, my dear nephew, in some happy hour, God allows me the honor of dancing at your wedding, I'll give you a much finer groom's gift than this! How I long to be worthy of seeing the beautiful, beloved bride whom the living God has destined for you! Only He, who lends us life, will reveal the joyful bride, may she be brought up in peace and happiness. Nothing comes before its time.

"Be healthy, do everything as I've written, and have a happy, joyful holiday as your faithful aunt wishes for you with her whole heart. Gitl-Reyzl Goldshteyn."

"What a marvel to hear such words," said Brayndl when Mirele finished reading. "Such a cultivated Jewess; a truly well-educated woman, as I'm a Jewish daughter! She's written quite a *megillah;* exactly as a person would talk. While you were reading, I believed Hershele's aunt stood here with us, or that I sat there with her in her home. That's a clever woman."

"See, and you said a young lady only needs a little writing skill," Mirele reminded her mother. "You see how good and fine it is when a woman can write a good letter in Yiddish?"

"And you see, my daughter, you study and study and still you can't compose such a fine letter. One has to be born with such a head and mind to write like that."

"Do my head and mind not please you, mother?" Mirele asked sharply. "Why didn't you provide me with better?"

"Of course you please me, child! I'm simply saying in general how fine it is that such a lovely letter can be written. One could kiss every word."

"Mama, if I had such a dear nephew as Hershele, I might write him an even lovelier letter," Mirele said. Then, suddenly embarrassed by her words, she quickly added, "I mean, if I were ever far away from you, dear Mama, I'd write you even better letters, prettier letters. Ah, Mama, would you be happy to get such letters from me?"

"No, my child, I'll never be separated from you," answered Brayndl with a heavy sigh. "Let people shower me with gold, I'll never let you leave me. Sad to say, what is my life, my world, without you? As long as I live, I'll have you here by my side, in my house. If God, blessed be He, sends you your destined mate, one who'll find favor in my eyes, he'll be my child too, and it will be twice as happy in my house as it is now. If your luck wakes up and shines on you, I'll give you everything I have—when your true destined love comes."

"How quickly she speaks of destined matches," Mirele said in an amused tone. "Tell me, instead, that tomorrow you'll go buy clothes for Hershele. Or better yet, ask for them to be brought here, and I'll choose. You know I have better taste than you," she said with a little laugh.

"Don't change the subject, my child. A time will come when your dear *besherter*—your destined one will arrive. A year from now, or at the latest, two—I can't wait for the happy day."

"Mama, give me back the money," Mirele answered angrily. "I'll go shopping myself if you don't want to. Don't worry, the storekeepers won't put anything over on me; I know the price of good clothes."

"But it won't do for you to go, my child. Let me; I'll go. Why deprive me of the mitzvah?"

"I'm afraid you'll go to Chaim Sefora's and ask him to give you goods as payment for an old debt. That will make them more expensive."

"Child, do you think I have no sense? I'll tell him, 'I'm paying cash, on faith.' Chaim Sefora won't sell his reputation for a ruble, not even for ten. Then I'll say to him, 'Let it be reckoned as if on consignment.' That way he'll provide the goods, and I'll hold on to Hershele's money. Why would you keep your mother from squaring an old debt?"

"But what if he refuses?"

"Then I won't have any alternative; I'll pay him the money."

"All right," agreed Mirele, convinced her mother would not hesitate.

In fact, Brayndl was pleased that Hershele had—supposedly—brought her his money. Now, she could finally settle an old debt.

That afternoon, Mirele was tenderly attentive to her mother, and that evening when Brayndl headed to bed so she could arise early the next morning and settle her debt with the tailor, Chaim Sefora, Mirele sat beside her for a few minutes and told her a pretty story.

The tale was about a prince who sought a wife who desired him not for his riches but for his merits. He disguised himself as a pauper and went wandering through his kingdom as a beggar. He was very handsome, and when he began singing, even the trees in the woods stopped rustling and bent to hear his sweet song.

One day he came into a town where there lived a great millionaire who had an only daughter, a very fine girl of marriageable age. But no match her father proposed was ever to her liking. When the beggar came and stood under her window to sing and beg for alms, the only daughter heard his sweet song. The melody moved her in every limb, and she ran to the window to see who sang so sweetly.

"Understand, Mama? The girl couldn't tear herself away," said Mirele. From that time forward, the millionaire's daughter began to burn with love for the poor man. She tried to forget him—she felt it beneath her dignity, in front of her friends, to be in love with a poor beggar. Every night he came to sing under her window, and one night, she had no more strength to resist. She fell on his neck and told him of her love. "But I'm a poor man," he said, "your rich parents will drive us away if you marry me!"

Still, she could no longer live without him, even if she'd have to become a pauper and go begging along with him from house to house. They soon married; when her father and family found out, they pressed the couple to separate. But she cried, "I'd rather die than be parted from him." Her father saw she was telling the truth, and doctors said she would indeed die without him. Having no choice, the father finally accepted the boy into the family. Imagine the father's great surprise and happiness when the poor beggar threw off his torn clothes and stood dressed gloriously as a prince!

"So Mama, what do you think? Was he glad his dear daughter fell in love with the beggar?"

"Of course he was happy, my child," Brayndl answered. "What then, did he not know that his daughter had happened upon good fortune?"

"But do you see, Mama, why she happened upon this good fortune? Because she'd understood his singing and not looked for riches, fine clothing, and expensive jewelry."

"Tell me, daughter, was the prince a Jew?" Brayndl asked.

"There are no Jewish princes," Mirele replied, "but there are Jewish children who, though poor, can become rich—from small and lowly, they can become great and famous. It can happen, Mama, that someone who seems to be poor, who we're ashamed of, suddenly takes on a great role in life, and now he's ashamed of us."

"Why are you telling me this, my child? Do you think I don't know that poverty and wealth lie in God's hands?"

"That's just what I'm saying," Mirele answered, and seeing her sleepy mother's eyes closing, she quietly left the bedroom.

*   *   *   *   *

Early the next morning, immediately after prayers, Hershele had a talk with the Vilner about the sages and great people he had mentioned the night before. Hershele admitted he yearned to learn more and that he'd already read one little book in Hebrew, the story of Amnon and Tamar.

The Vilner was happy he'd finally found someone among his friends with whom he could discuss the novel *Love of Zion,* which had made a deep impression on his heart as well. He told Hershele to read other books by the same author as quickly as possible.

"It seems to me you could find these books in the house where you take your Wednesday meal," he said. "I've heard Brayndl's husband was among the Enlightened and that many of his books are still there. Give it a try; ask. If they let you look at his bookcase, I bet you'll find them all there."

"If they're there, I'm sure Brayndl will agree," Hershele said.

"Listen," the Vilner said, "the books are good for waking one who's asleep, but such works don't contain the remedy to give strength to those who are already awakened and can stand on their own two feet. Therefore, you should first read the books I've told you about—so you can awaken from your poor boy's sleep, look around you, and stop laboring pointlessly forever.

"Then afterwards, you can look at other books, ones that actually stand a man on his feet. It's too late for me; I'll never become respectable. You, however, can still achieve something for yourself, particularly since God has given you such an instrument, such a voice. Wherever you show up, they'll grab you!"

"Why do you say it's too late for you?" Hershele asked with compassion. "You study more cleverly than I do. I always have to work to catch up with you."

"Too late, brother," the Vilner answered with a sigh. "I don't have any of your merits. And besides, I'm five or six years older. True, I know a bit about everything, but I'm not an expert on anything. My whole life is without order as is my studying. I often look at myself as one who's crawling in a swamp; a man sinking deeper every hour but without the heart or strength to save himself. I haven't the strength to tear myself from the study house. It's too late. I'll remain a simple *melamud,* a teacher of little children, a poor man, a ruin. But you, your powers are in Torah. For you the whole world is open, and I predict you'll travel and achieve great success."

"Let's both go," Hershele pleaded. "I promise to share everything with you, like a brother."

"I thank you, but you must travel alone," the Vilner answered. "I'll only ask you this: I already know I'll never rise in status, and I know further, that you will someday become one of the great people. Hershele, if my poverty ever brings me to it, if some day I need your help, please hear my plea. Remember then how we sat here now in the study house; remember what we're talking about. Brother, don't forget your friend from Vilna, who gave you the advice to tear yourself away from here."

Hershele's heart was moved by the Vilner's words, and he wanted to tell him about his thoughts from the previous night, but was interrupted by a yeshiva boy who shouted, "Hershele, you're being called to your Wednesday meal."

In that moment, Brayndl's serving maid came in and said, "The mistress requests you come now. A letter containing money has arrived from your uncle!"

"You have an uncle, Hershele?" the Vilner asked. From his conversation with Mirele, Hershele knew who his "good uncle and dear aunt" were, and replied, "I have an uncle, a very dear and faithful one."

"If he sends money, he's certainly faithful and beloved," the Vilner remarked. "How much money?"

"Wait, I myself don't yet know how much," Hershele answered, and was immediately on his way to Brayndl's.

"Silly boy, why didn't you tell us you have such a good uncle and such a clever and faithful aunt?" Brayndl asked as soon as Hershele said hello. Suddenly his face turned red from embarrassment; it was hard for him to answer calmly with a lie.

"Why are you embarrassed, child? I wish all our friends had such a fortune to be embarrassed about. I really shouldn't flatter you, but believe me, I've always thought you must be descended from a fine family. Hearing my Mirele, let her be healthy, read your aunt's letter gave me great pleasure to see I wasn't mistaken about you. She must be a dear woman. Is she your mother's sister?"

"A sister," he barely managed to get out without being sure of what he was saying.

"Your mother is long dead?"

"Eight years already, rest in peace."

"And your uncle, may he have long years, he's really rich?"

"Once he was quite rich. Now, I don't know."

"May God help him, he's certainly a fine Jew!" Brayndl said, and would have asked more questions about his family, but Mirele came in with an armful of merchandise and rescued him from her mother's interrogation.

"Do you like this coat?" she asked quickly, winking at him so he'd understand. "From the thirty-five rubles your aunt sent, Mama paid out eighteen rubles and sixty kopecks. So you'll have it all: a suit with a summer coat, as your aunt wrote. Gitl-Reyzl, her name is. Look, I remember! She's your mother's sister, I think?"

"Long years to her," Brayndl added. "Your mother will intercede in heaven for both you and her dear sister who hasn't deserted you."

Hershele heard the reminders in Mirele's words, but he found it difficult to calmly play his role. He was ashamed before Brayndl and before himself, and couldn't lift his eyes.

"Why don't you thank me for my trouble?" Mirele asked with a friendly smile to encourage him. Hershele raised his eyes and looked at her.

"Silly boy, she doesn't actually want your thanks," Brayndl said. "What, do you think she doesn't know a mitzvah requires no thanks?"

"No, I really want to be thanked!" said Mirele playfully.

"Are my thanks worth as much, then, as the trouble you went to on my behalf?" Hershele asked, finally finding something to say.

"Oh, your gratitude is very worthy," Mirele answered coquettishly. "Don't think we don't know who you are. We know, and we hope some day you'll be rich and happy again. Perhaps in the future you'll even be embarrassed by your friendship with us."

"If you think I could ever be embarrassed by your friendship or forget your loving kindness, my thanks are worth nothing at all," he answered earnestly.

"'Where there's Torah, there's wisdom,'" said Brayndl happily. "He knows how to answer properly."

"Then I suppose you are indeed guilty for thanking me," said Mirele smiling sweetly.

"I thank you; I thank you a thousand times," said Hershele. "I'll be guilty of thanking you forever!"

He also tried to thank Brayndl, who replied, "I certainly do not desire thanks, my son. Let my eyes see as many good things in my own child as I see in you—as I wish for you."

When Mirele left the room, Brayndl said, "What do you say, isn't my Mirele a diamond? You don't know how she pestered me until I gave her exactly what she wanted. You can depend on her taste; she knows quality."

Just then the tailor arrived and measured Hershele from head to toe. "A little longer and wider," Brayndl ordered. "One doesn't wear such expensive clothes for only one day. One wears them again and again."

Mirele, however, told him to cut the clothes exactly to the current fashion. If she'd wanted them made as her mother suggested, she'd have given the job to Berl Lopetnik, not him.

"What do you want?" the tailor asked Hershele.

"Don't listen to her!" Brayndl said before Hershele could answer. "That's how she'd sew a dress for herself: narrow and tight, good to wear a couple of times and then sell cheaply. I tell you, one can make shorter from longer, but one can't make longer from shorter!"

"But just see what your aunt writes," Mirele said, handing the letter to Hershele. "Look, she wants the suit cut fashionably so if you have to go home suddenly, people won't laugh at you."

"I want to obey my aunt," Hershele said, shyly expressing his opinion. "It's her money; why not obey her?"

In the end, the tailor agreed with everyone: he'd cut the clothes as Mirele requested, but leave a large hem for Brayndl. "I sew, praise God, for the finest householders," he said, "even for noble-men. Don't worry, I won't ruin your precious wares."

"See that you leave a big hem," Brayndl ordered again, "and don't forget to bring back the left-over fabric!"

"Listen, Brayndl," the tailor assured her, "I have a hundred pieces left over from the clothing I've already cut. Don't worry. I'll cut the garment and bring it; then we'll talk."

"Don't forget: this is a poor boy's blood money. You are also earning a mitzvah! Bring the suit, but not too near the holidays in case an alteration or repair is needed. One can't be expected to do that oneself."

"Good day, Brayndl," the tailor answered, taking the goods under his arm and leaving.

While Brayndl was still standing by the door, chatting with the tailor, Mirele had time to tell Hershele to keep his spirits up; all would turn out well. He promised gratefully, and then asked if he could borrow a book? Mirele immediately asked her mother for the key to the bookcase.

"What do you want with the key?" Brayndl asked.

"He wants to borrow a book."

"You see, my daughter, the difference between Hershele and another? He's not enthusiastic about the new clothes, but a book! Give him the key. He can find my Passover prayer book and the Haggadahs at the same time."

Mirele took Hershele to a side room, opened the glass doors of a great bookcase full of books, and told him to find whatever he wanted. As his eyes raced over the shelves, Mirele began reading aloud some of the titles. Hershele gently corrected her pronuncia-tion of Hebrew words and explained to her the contents of each book. The holy books were all good, familiar friends; not one was unknown to him. As Mirele listened, she wondered how a person could study and remember so many large volumes.

"What's the main purpose of studying all these books?" she asked.

"To become a rabbi, a great sage," Hershele replied simply.

"And nothing more?"

"Nothing more," he answered with a sigh, as if a heavy feeling tortured him. He'd expended so much energy on so many books; had spent his health and years of his life on studying them. Yet now he was seeking out different books that would open his eyes to a whole new world.

Finally, on the bottom shelf, he beheld many books with titles he'd never seen before. "All the books on the upper shelves, I've studied day and night—but they've led me nowhere," he said in a serious tone. "The ones below I've never seen before; perhaps in them I'll find what I'm beginning to seek."

"There is another bookcase over there," said Mirele, pointing across the room. "But they're not Jewish books, Hershele. With holy books, perhaps one can become a sage, but with the others, one can become educated and cultured. I give them all to you, and hope that with your ability to learn from all those holy books, you won't find these new ones too difficult. I just hope you find what you're looking for."

"Mirele, I must absorb their ideas," he said, "and I will!"

A few moments later, Brayndl called her daughter to lunch. As they sat together at the table, Mirele asked, "Mama, why haven't you invited Hershele to eat with us? Please call him in—and also invite him to Passover."

"I'm not ignoring him, Mirele. Of course he'll eat with us. But I think the seder will go better if we invite an older Jew to sit at our table. What do you say?"

"Hershele knows more than your old Jews," Mirele replied forcefully. "Let him come to us for the entire week of Passover. Show him you're truly a good and faithful friend. You'll see, your kindness to him will make you proud and happy."

"Yes, let him eat healthy. He'll come to us for Passover," said Brayndl as she went to get Hershele.

Hershele let himself be invited. Brayndl's kindness was hard to bear, but he finally agreed when Mirele came in and asked for his consent. At the table Brayndl invited him for the whole of Passover, and Mirele said she'd be asking the four questions, so he should come prepared with good answers.

Brayndl was proud of her dear child's goodness and comfortable tone as she watched her talking with Hershele. She'd always believed—and people had told her—that Mirele was a truly wonderful child, clever and educated, but a bit too standoffish and proud. Now she saw this was no longer true. On the contrary, here she was talking with a yeshiva boy as if she were his sister and he a member of the family. This made Brayndl very happy.

"Don't forget to come for dinner," Mirele said as he was leaving. "For all of Passover. Mama won't let you eat away. Ask him, Mama, yourself," she turned to her mother. "He doesn't believe me."

Brayndl had no alternative and promised he could have meals with them through the end of Passover. "Remember," Mirele said again. "If not, Mama will be very offended with you, and I'll be angry as well!"

ELEVEN

Borekh's wife waited at home until noon, though it was Thursday and she really needed to go to the meat market. She had planned to give Hershele his mid-day meal and announced that from this day forward he would no longer be eating charity meals with other householders; he would eat at her house. "Sooner or later he will be one of our own," she told her husband. "Enough of this wandering about; enough humiliation at other people's tables."

But the clock struck 12:00, then 12:30, and Hershele still hadn't arrived. Soreh-Feyge sat staring through the window, anxiously hoping to see him walking down the street, but he wasn't to be seen. She grew sad.

Her mother noticed and consoled her, "He's embarrassed, naturally. He's no fool. It isn't suitable for him to come here as a yeshiva boy for his charity meal. His meal should be sent to him in the study house. Tonight, when your father has time, I'll send him to invite Hershele to spend Passover with us."

Soreh-Feyge grew calmer and soon prepared a fine meal for Hershele and sent it to the study house. When the food arrived, the yeshiva boys ran to tell Hershele that his in-laws had sent him a meal. But in vain—they couldn't find Hershele anywhere.

Aroused by the aroma from the meat and rich *tsimes,* the hungry schoolboys decided to cheat both Hershele and Borekh. "He's not fool enough to give himself away for a little *tsimes,*" they convinced themselves.

"Hershele's upstairs in the women's *shul,*" one of the boys told the serving maid. "He's too shy to come down. He asks that I take him the meal and that you wait here for the empty dishes."

The maid handed them the meal. Ten minutes later, the boys brought back the empty dishes and asked the maid to thank Borekh's wife, in Hershele's name, "for the wonderful meal which he very much enjoyed."

Borekh's wife received these thanks happily, and showed Soreh-Feyge the empty dishes. "See, my daughter, in the study house, where he isn't shy, he eats—no evil eye—in a completely different manner. I don't begrudge him a bit."

"Certainly he didn't eat this all by himself," Soreh-Feyge answered. She didn't want her mother to think Hershele was such a glutton. "His friends probably helped him out."

The serving maid, wanting to gain more approval from her mistress, lied and said she'd seen Hershele eating all the food himself. "He bade me thank you personally," she said.

"You're lying!" Soreh-Feyge shouted at her. "You think I don't know he can't eat that much?"

"What are you worrying about?" said her mother. "He ate, he shared it with his friends, that's fine. You'll see, next time I'll send twice as much."

"Will he be with us for Shabbes?" Soreh-Feyge begged.

"He'll be here, daughter, don't despair," consoled her mother as she headed off to the meat market.

An hour later, Hershele was back from Brayndl's and immediately began reading the new books with the Vilner. He didn't know lunch had been brought to him, and none of the other boys said a word. That night he was off again to Brayndl's for dinner, though he wasn't hungry, and again the yeshiva boys helped themselves to the meal Borekh's wife sent.

The Slutsker said, "We're doing a mitzvah for him! Let's hope he doesn't follow in the Vilner's path. If he does, Borekh the butcher is going to look around one day, see the mistake he's made, and say, 'Woe is me that I have given my bread to an ignorant man.'"

When Hershele returned that evening, one of the boys who hadn't gotten any of Borekh's dinner, told him of his friends' deception. But instead of being angry, Hershele, who was in such a good mood, just laughed along with the others, and swore to his friends that Borekh the butcher was completely in error. That he, Hershele, hadn't for one instant considered becoming his son-in-law. "If it would help," he said, "I'd fast for three days in a row to separate myself from him."

"You're a fool," said one of the yeshiva boys. "He can't drag you to the wedding canopy against your will. So what are you afraid of? And if necessary, you could always run away."

"Thus speaks a thief who must run away from his deeds," replied Hershele. "I won't run. I'm very grateful to Borekh. He's always treated me like family. Honestly, if I were suddenly wealthy, I'd give him all my riches if he'd only forgive me and remain as good a friend as he's always been."

"But of what are you guilty?" asked the Vilner, consoling him. "It's the matchmaker who's guilty, may his name be blotted out. No telling what he's said. In the meantime, you've fasted already today on his account, may Borekh forgive you!"

But Hershele hadn't fasted—far from it—but he was afraid to admit to his friends that he'd eaten at Brayndl's. To keep his secret from being revealed, he remained silent.

"Children," called out one of the students, "Passover is coming. Let's roust out all the *chametz* from our boxes, chests, and secret hiding places. Whoever has bread, bring it here."

In only a few minutes, they had gathered together several pieces of dry bread, bagels, and a few rolls. A couple of boys also found a bit of herring and some pickles. They put a curtain over a table and forced Hershele to go wash up so they could all eat together. He added a few kopecks to buy more herring and a couple quarts of *kvass;* and when everything was assembled, they had a feast worthy of King Solomon.

The friends began singing, and the Vilner shared a bit of Torah. Hershele sang and the group traded jokes. Everyone was merry, and even the Slutsker reconciled with the Vilner.

When the festivities ended, and Hershele and the Vilner were gone, the boys all agreed to tell the matchmaker to switch things up. Instead of Hershele, he should propose the Slutsker to Borekh, and somehow they'd find a way to ensure Hershele would be Brayndl's choice as a bridegroom. Even the Slutsker gave his half-hearted consent.

On Friday, Hershele had no time or desire to hear the secrets his friends were whispering among themselves. He spent the whole day sitting in the women's *shul,* diligently reading the new books. He even forgot to think of an excuse for Borekh, in case he were asked to come for Passover.

Borekh, on his part, could barely wait for the approach of evening, when he would bring Hershele home as his wife had commanded the previous day. But as soon as he glimpsed Hershele during evening prayers, the boy ran away in the middle of the *shmone esrey.* Hershele waited in a corner of the study house courtyard until the crowd thinned and the coast was clear, then he headed straight to Brayndl's. He had already sent word to the household where he usually took his Shabbes meal that he would not be coming to eat.

Though Borekh looked up and down for him, and asked if anyone had seen him, he could not find Hershele anywhere. Greatly irritated, he went home without the future bridegroom.

"I told you not to wait until the last moment," his wife shouted. "He's completely in the right to go eat his usual Shabbes meal. When people invite a bridegroom to their house, they shouldn't call him to the table like some poverty case."

"You know what kind of day I had?" Borekh complained. "The cursed *shochet* came with a question while the rabbi was at a *bris*. Here it is, Shabbes coming on, women are waiting in the meat market, and there's no meat, because the ritual slaughterer has a question! And what is the question? What a joke! When the rabbi finally shows up, he slaves over it, he begins to huff and puff, rummages through all his holy books, wrinkles up his forehead, and barely has enough strength to get out the word: 'Kosher!' So, dear wife, why are you offended? Should I have skipped going to the ritual bath before Shabbes? Don't worry if Messiah is born a day later. Passover's almost here; where else will the boy go?"

His wife was swiftly consoled, but Soreh-Feyge sat sadly at the table. Her heart told her something wasn't right. When her mother tried comforting her after supper, she said, "I think he's embarrassed to come in his poor clothing. You'll see: he won't come for Passover either."

Soreh-Feyge's mother soothed her and promised that her father would take Hershele for new clothes—the best and most beautiful—right after Shabbes. She then went to talk the plan over with Borekh.

The following day, the yeshiva boys met with Shlomo the matchmaker and proposed their plan to him, promising him everything good if he'd upend Borekh's marriage agreement and sub-stitute the Slutsker for Hershele.

"Impossible!" exclaimed the matchmaker. "Borekh wants Rachel, not Leah, understand? And Brayndl can offer a dowry of five thousand rubles. Who knows, maybe even ten thousand! She's looking for a rich man's son for her princess; and I can tell you for certain, Brayndl won't consider Hershele for a moment. This is my business. You think I don't know what people want?"

"What happens," asked one of the students, "if Rachel doesn't want to be taken by Jacob? What would be the outcome if Rachel were to say, 'Absolutely not, I won't have him!'"

"What? Hershele doesn't want the match with the butcher's daughter? Why wouldn't he want it?" Shlomo asked.

"Because he doesn't; he doesn't want it! Nu, what can you do about it?"

"Then we must force him until he wants it. Woe to such a rascal if he says he doesn't want it," said the matchmaker.

"But he absolutely doesn't!" all the yeshiva boys said together.

"But how is this your concern, scoundrels?" Shlomo asked angrily. But the yeshiva boys did not back down, and the argument continued for fully half an hour with the two sides wrangling and insulting each other.

The matchmaker cursed them, and the boys in turn insisted: "Though the world may be turned upside down, Hershele will not be Borekh's son-in-law!"

They said this more for revenge on the matchmaker for his curses than for Hershele's good. They also took pains to ensure that Borekh would not get near Hershele. They worried that Hershele, fearful of seeming disobedient to an elder, would weaken from embarrassment and change his mind.

But that evening, Borekh spotted Hershele and grabbed him. "Tell me, Hershele," he asked, "why have you so offended me by not coming to us for Shabbes?"

"Why should I come to you?" Hershele replied, then looked away in embarrassment. Borekh, seeing the look on Hershele's face, thought he was offended for not having been invited earlier.

"You're right," he answered amiably. "May the ritual slaughter's head be twisted—he twisted my head so, I didn't have time to invite you as I should have. So now I'm telling you, tomorrow, God willing, you should come to us after prayers. I'll take you for new clothes. Meanwhile, you'll come to us at least for the Passover holiday. Afterwards, we'll all see what's needed."

"Thank you, Reb Borekh, for your good intentions. Believe me, I'm very sorry you've misunderstood me so thoroughly. I'm not so poor and alone, God forbid. Just this past Thursday, I hired the tailor to make me a new suit."

Confused, Borekh stared at him. "What do you mean?" he asked.

Hershele didn't have the nerve to tell Borekh to his face that there was no engagement, so he remained silent.

Borekh waited in vain for a reply, then finally said, "Then I'll buy you a fine watch and chain. My wife, long life to her, is really a sage. She figured you must be offended because I didn't invite you in advance for Shabbes. So now, Hershele, with plenty of advance notice, I'm inviting you to come for all of Passover. Do you hear? For the whole holiday. You can give up your charity meals; it doesn't suit me for you to be eating on charity to the very last minute. If you like, you can come eat with us on all the days preceding Passover as well. If you worry what people might say, I'll have breakfast and lunch brought to you at the study house."

"Thank you, Reb Borekh," Hershele answered with a truly broken heart. "I can't even come to you for Passover. Brayndl already asked me on Wednesday to come to her from then on, and I promised her I would. I've been eating at her home ever since."

"What's this you say? My wife told me you were embarrassed to come for your Thursday meal, so she sent food to the study house," Borekh said with growing agitation.

"It's true, your wife sent food, but I don't know who ate it. I certainly didn't, because I ate at Brayndl's."

"We're not talking about Wednesday, *shlemiel;* I'm asking you about Passover, understand?"

"I can't, Reb Borekh. I've eaten meals at Brayndl's for as long as I've been coming to you. She's always made me feel at home, and she herself went to the store and bargained with the tailor about the clothes he'll sew for me. How could I be ungrateful to her?"

"To the devil with that cursed woman!" Borekh shouted angrily. "You *must* come to us for Passover."

"I must go to her, Reb Borekh, and I will," said Hershele decisively.

"You're a stubborn child. I beg you—or perhaps you're feeling regret?"

"I don't have anything to regret."

"I don't either," Borekh said a little more softly, not understanding Hershele.

"Let's remain friends," Hershele said trying to calm him. "You know, Reb Borekh, a person isn't born under a stone. I do have relatives, and they have an opinion, too. Especially since they haven't abandoned me."

"What's this I'm hearing?" Borekh shouted, taken aback. "This is not what you told the matchmaker."

"Why do you believe the matchmaker?" Hershele asked in anguish. "He didn't tell you the truth."

"What are you saying, Hershele?"

"I'm saying the matchmaker is a liar!"

"Is this how you show your gratitude?"

"Who's guilty here, Reb Borekh? If I could, I'd thank you with my life. This has already brought me so much suffering."

Hershele's quiet and earnest tone cooled Borekh's surprise and anger a little. "People have put you up to this," he said, softening. "You're not an impudent fellow. You'll come to us for Passover, even if the whole world stands on its head! And then we'll see. Have a good Shabbes, Hershele. I'm not angry with you. On the contrary, it gives me pleasure that you're not a pushover."

Hershele, suddenly feeling like a heavy weight had dropped from his shoulders, answered happily, "Good Shabbes."

When he returned home, Borekh didn't share his aggravation with his wife and daughter. But the next day when he met with the matchmaker, he let him have it.

"Reb Borekh, hear me out," Shlomo the matchmaker insisted. "I haven't been such a sinful Jew, God forbid, as to flat out lie to you, especially as it wouldn't serve me in the slightest. I'll run to Hershele and find out what's going on with him. Why should you worry about what he wants? Let me handle it," Shlomo assured him as he headed to the study house.

"What's the story with you, my fine fellow?" he asked Hershele as soon as he found him.

"What story are you talking about?" Hershele asked.

"The way you spoke to Borekh, an in-law who'll make you happy?"

"Why do you come nagging me about in-laws?" Hershele answered back with spirit. "You can arrange betrothals as you please—but I don't want to hear about it."

"Hear his arrogance!" the matchmaker said growing angry. "Do you really believe it when your pals, those loafers, say you're suitable to be Brayndl's son-in-law? You beast! What are you; who are you? So what if you can study a little and sing a little; where's your fine family background? When I was a boy I knew more than you do. And what kind of match did I make for myself? My bride was a schoolteacher's daughter with a hundred rubles for a dowry, a year of monetary support, and that's it! And in case you think I was deceived, on the contrary; they got the worse deal: for five years I was a burden on my father-in-law and never earned two kopecks. And what am I now? A poor man! Let my enemies choose bridegrooms from the study house! Here's what you're forgetting my young friend: if one has a wife, one needs work to sustain her. With what will you start out? Will you, too, teach little children? Woe to the girl who's destined to be a schoolteacher's wife!

"If a matchmaker were to come to me today and say, 'Reb Shlomo, I have two grooms to propose for your daughter: one is Hershele the yeshiva boy, the other is a simple tailor.' Who do you think I'd grab? The tailor. Why? It's simple: the tailor would at least be able to provide bread for my daughter. But with you, I can't even guarantee there will be bread at your table, God forbid! I don't wish that for you, but I call it as I see it.

"Aren't I myself envious of even the humblest tradesman? What good is it that people call me 'Reb Shlomo?' What do I gain from studying the Gemara for so many years? Barely a living of sixty or seventy rubles a season. Do you think it's in expectation of luxury that I run after matches and haggle until my throat is dry? It's privation that drives me: my wife's curses and my children crying for food!

"And why am I arguing with you right now? In order to have a few pounds of meat in the holiday pot, the meat Borekh won't give me if you stubbornly hold out. See, if this were a bad deal for you, you'd have a right to complain. After all, you're not obligated to help me earn my keep if the match is unsuitable. But I know, Hershele, that it's you, not Borekh, who's getting the bargain here. It's your good luck that he's prospered as a butcher and wants a lad with Torah and all the trimmings. Don't be a fool! Grab this opportunity with both hands and forget about anyone else. Here's a good bride, a bit of good fortune for her husband. She won't wait for you to bring in the money from your work; she'll work hard for you instead of you working for her. You'll be supported like royalty! Send to me, Master of the Universe, such meat for my children to eat—at least on holidays—as is eaten at Borekh's house day and night!"

"Reb Shlomo, believe me, I understand what you're saying," answered Hershele. "You're absolutely right in everything. But I'm not obligated to report my thoughts to you. Tell Borekh I'll be forever grateful, but I will never be his son-in-law."

"I don't wish you ill," the matchmaker said. "I only want you to promise you'll at least eat with Borekh at Passover. How can it bother you to have a fine Passover meal with his family? Don't be an idiot; eat and drink where it is provided. After that, it's your choice to go there again. Who can force you?"

"I never promised you anything," Hershele answered. "All your talk is in vain. I won't be going to Borekh's for Passover."

"Robber!" Shlomo shouted in despair. "You stab me without a knife! I haven't got even the beginnings of a Passover meal: no matzah, no meat, no potatoes! All my hopes were in Borekh, and then you go ruin everything! What is this? Aren't I a Jew? My wife and children shouldn't eat during Passover? Why have you no pity, you thief?"

"Is this my fault?" Hershele asked.

"Whose fault is it, then? Is it me who doesn't want the match? I wish I could have the kind of Passover you'd enjoy at his home."

"Leave me alone!" Hershele finally said as he got up from the bench and headed for the door.

The matchmaker ran after him. "You know what I say to you? I agree!" Shlomo began again in supplication. "I myself can change Borekh's mind. Engagements are made and also broken. The same mouth that said, 'Hershele is good,' can also say, 'he's not right at all.' But meanwhile, until after the holidays, please go to him. How can it hurt you to be there? Meanwhile, I'll get a few pounds of meat, and perhaps a couple of rubles for wine and potatoes. As you see I'm a Jew; I'll make it up to you, Hershele! I can put in a favorable word for you with Brayndl; she listens to me."

"I can't help you, Reb Shlomo," Hershele answered coldly as he walked away.

"Remember, Hershele, you'll regret this!" the matchmaker shouted after him.

Hershele didn't look back, as if the words weren't meant for him, but his heart ached. "What do they want from me, Master of the Universe?" he pleaded. "Am I obliged to sell myself or deceive Borekh so the matchmaker won't suffer on Passover? Why don't you, Master of the Universe, send him a different occupation? Why does he have to make Passover from his matchmaker's earnings?"

Even darker thoughts ran through his mind. He gathered from the matchmaker's words that he'd once been a yeshiva boy himself and a fine scholar. And this is how he ended up: such a pauper now, poor thing, that he thinks it's acceptable to bully, swindle, swear oaths, and lie, just so he can survive in his profession.

"And what will become of me?" Hershele asked himself. "Perhaps I'd be even more of a pauper than Reb Shlomo, if it weren't for Mirele, who wants to make me happy and urges me to travel and improve my station." This thought gave him new strength to work hard, and he suddenly felt an urge to find a place far away where he could become an important person.

When he finally arrived at Brayndl's, Mirele greeted him with a fond look. Brayndl, like a faithful aunt, treated him like family, and Hershele began to feel happy again. He forgot about Borekh and the matchmaker, and only one thought remained: the sooner he traveled away to better himself, the sooner he could return a successful man.

With this in mind, he headed back to the study house and diligently studied the new books, as he once had studied the ancient Gemara. Now, as before, Mirele was the reason for his diligence, but his lust for learning was also growing stronger.

A week passed, and Passover eve finally arrived. Right after the "burning of the *chametz*," the tailor delivered his new clothes to Brayndl's, and the serving maid called Hershele to be fitted. The tailor helped him take off the old clothes and put on the new ones. It was hard for him to bear this: in his whole life no one had ever helped him put on a garment. Now both the tailor and his assistant were pulling and buttoning, as if Hershele didn't have hands to do it himself.

But the garments were so finely made and expensive, one had to be careful putting them on. They seemed like stranger's clothes, not his own. He forbid the tailor to give an opinion. When the tailor wanted to know if the work was well done, Hershele took him by the hand and led him to where Mirele and Brayndl were waiting. The tailor tugged at the right hem, then the left, then lifted the collar a little closer to the neck. He straightened Hershele's arms and turned him to face the critics as the blood rushed to Hershele's face.

"What do you say?" the tailor asked proudly.

"Good!" Mirele called out, and she saw Hershele shine.

"Good? What do you mean by that?" asked the tailor. "Nothing could be better!"

"I'm aggravated," said Brayndl indignantly. "This seems sewn for a child: narrow and short. With as much material as you had, couldn't you have made it longer and wider?"

"Why are you worrying, Brayndl?" the tailor asked authoritatively. "This is how it should be. I'm not a Jew if you could see a finer suit in Paris."

"But just look how it pulls across the sleeve," Brayndl pointed. "Woe is me, it seems he can't even lift his arm."

The tailor grabbed Hershele by both arms and lifted first the right and then the left. He then bent the boy over like a juggler, stuck his broad arms under the coat up to the chest and shouted in triumph, "So what do you say now? Still think it's too narrow and tight? I did a great job. Look at how wide the hems are!"

Taking her hand, he showed her the hems and soothed her. "What are you worrying about? It wasn't for nothing that your daughter Mirele chose to call on me. Forgive me, but she knows the fashions better than you."

All the while Hershele felt clumsy and embarrassed. The tailor commanded him: "Stand up straight! Raise your right arm, now your left! Bend over!" He turned and twisted Hershele on all sides as if he were an officer and Hershele his soldier.

"All right already, enough with the military drill!" he told the tailor, chagrined. "It's fine. I think it's perfect, let me be!"

"No, they need to see what a picture you are. See how it lays?" the tailor asked, not letting go. "Come to the mirror and look. See, at least you're not at all as you were before!"

Hershele was terribly offended by the tailor's words and suddenly felt the weight of his entire desolation.

At the mirror, the tailor pulled off Hershele's cap because it didn't go with the new outfit, and Brayndl declared, "It'd be better to tear it up!"

"No, wear it in good health!" Mirele said with a charming smile.

"I thank you," Hershele answered politely, "though I know you don't want me to express thanks."

When Hershele went to the other room to change, the tailor clicked his tongue and said, "Isn't he a real monarch? A king's son, as I live and breathe!"

"Clothing makes the man," Brayndl said and began haggling over the price of the suit.

Once he had changed, Hershele began gathering his new clothes to take back to the yeshiva, but Mirele stopped him. "I don't want to give you up now," she said. "Passover eve is also Passover. You must eat with us starting now."

"Yes!" agreed Brayndl. "Why must you go back to the study house? Stay with us—you can help prepare the seder and purify the new dishes. What more must you do at the study house today?"

"We have enough rooms," Mirele said enthusiastically. "Come, see, I have prepared a room where you can stay until the end of Passover. There are books; you can read and study to your heart's content. And we'll be happier, too. Isn't it true, Mama?"

"It's really so!" Brayndl agreed. "You've spent the whole year in the study house; it's enough. Even the demons in *Gehennah* are resting for the whole month of Nissan, so why, my son, shouldn't you rest your limbs at least for the whole of Passover in a bed with real sheets and blankets? You'll be our dear guest."

Brayndl hadn't considered what was hidden in her heart. Yet since the evening when Mirele had read her Hershele's aunt's letter, he had become much dearer to her, as if he were her own child.

An hour later, Hershele was eating lunch with them. Brayndl told him not to be embarrassed and to eat hearty. "The day is already quite long," she said. "One can get very hungry waiting for the seder."

After the meal, Mirele went out to purchase some new things for herself and her mother to honor the holiday, and also to buy for Hershele what his outfit was still lacking. Meanwhile, as Hershele was sitting by the bookshelf deeply engrossed in a new book, he didn't notice as Brayndl came into the room with an apron full of nuts, apples, and cinnamon.

"Haven't you studied enough this whole year? Do something else for a change! Here, I've brought you nuts, apples, and cinnamon. Shell the nuts, peel the apples, grind the cinnamon, then pound it all together. We'll have *charoset* for the seder, and enough to share with the neighbors—it's my mitzvah not to be stingy with it."

Hershele was happy to help, and in a few minutes had completed all the tasks. When Brayndl tasted the *charoset,* she praised him: "This is wonderful. People in *Yisroel* would eat this!"

He demanded more work, and Brayndl honored him with filling the candleholders and purifying the new dishes. She showed him how to set the seder table, and gave him other odd jobs that were neither difficult nor demeaning. He did it all swiftly and well, and there was no limit to Brayndl's satisfaction.

"A man in the house," she said, "is a light in the house! All my good friends should have men in their homes; and whoever wishes me evil, let her be lonely and without the pleasure of having a man helping and preparing everything as it should be."

By the time Mirele returned, Hershele felt so at home that he was no longer shy about talking to her in her mother's presence.

"Did you prepare everything so beautifully?" Mirele asked.

"Yes, I did it all!" he answered proudly.

Mirele laughed and shook her head. "Come here and I'll show you how to do it properly," she said, as she immediately began to rearrange everything on the table. "Now, isn't that prettier?" she asked.

"Don't be discouraged, Hershele," Brayndl consoled him. "You can study a thousand times better than she can!"

"Mama, may I have permission to study with Hershele?"

"When would he have time for that?"

"During Passover, Mama. You'll see, I'll learn. I'll study Chumash," Mirele said turning to him. "Will you study with me, Hershele?"

"With pleasure," he replied.

"Good, it's settled; tomorrow we begin. I can do it, I can study with you!" Mirele said happily.

"And now, Mama, I've bought everything you need for the holiday except a hat. A hat you must buy for yourself!" And with these words, Mirele began unwrapping the packages and showing her mother the flowers, the lace, the scarf, and the other trifles she'd bought for her.

"What do I need all this for? Just to spend money?" Brayndl complained. "She thinks her mother is still a young woman!"

"To me, Mama, you are still a young woman and a very pretty one, may you live another one hundred and twenty years. Why should I stint when you're never stingy with me!"

"You at least understand how to flatter your mother!" Brayndl said, refusing to waste any more time looking over the other trifles.

TWELVE

In the study house just before evening prayers, Hershele's friends almost didn't recognize him in his new clothes. He hardly recognized himself. His heart felt more secure in its happiness. The new clothes called out to him, "We're proof you weren't born to the same luck as your poor comrades. You aren't like them!" Looking at the others' poor clothes hurt him deeply. He felt happy and wanted happiness for them as well.

They gathered around gazing jealously at him, petting the new attire from overcoat to undergarments. "Wear them in good health," they blessed him. Even the Slutsker wished him well and told him that he, the Slutsker, would be eating at Borekh's on the first day of Passover.

"'A righteous person may be saved from one trouble, but another will soon follow,'" remarked the Vilner in a Gemara chant. "You'd better beware of Borekh, Hershele. We think you're beyond hopeless in his eyes."

Another boy quoted from Proverbs, "'When God is pleased with a man's ways, even his enemies will make peace with him.' God can make friendship from hatred. You'll see, Hershele, Borekh will remain your good friend."

Hershele asked how it happened that Borekh had taken the Slutsker for the holiday.

"Simple," said one of the yeshiva boys. "Ten times he comes asking for you today. So I told him, 'Everybody wants Hershele, but nobody asks for the Slutsker. What a fair and a good deed, Reb Borekh, to take him for at least the first day.' And before I could get it all out of my mouth, Borekh—having no alternative—called the Slutsker to come for seder. What do you care? If the Slutsker just gets a toehold, all will turn out right."

This account gave Hershele pleasure, but his heart still felt Borekh's anger. He imagined the family's disappointment when they saw the Slutsker arrive instead of him.

Borekh himself had not thought it all through. He took the Slutsker because Hershele's friend asked him to. "And I'll even take three or four more yeshiva boys for Passover," he told himself, "but Hershele must come, too. Let Brayndl suffer a sickness for as long as she's ruining my holiday. She thinks she's found a new little 'Savior' in him? We'll see about that!"

So again, at evening prayers, Borekh approached Hershele and invited him home. "What have you got against me, Hershele?" he complained. "Have I done something wrong to you? Has my wife or someone from my family, God forbid, offended you? Why are you causing me all this aggravation, not coming home with me when I beg you?"

"I have nothing against you or your family, Reb Borekh. On the contrary, I'll never forget your loving kindness and friendship. But Brayndl has also never offended me. She's been kind and treated me like family. Besides, she asked me first. How can I then offend her and not go for seder after I promised?"

"But her invitation can't mean as much as ours," Borekh blurted out. "She invites you simply as an acquaintance. My invitation means something quite different! You're not a child; you shouldn't pretend ignorance. Tell me yourself, doesn't it seem improper for you not to come to us at Passover? Come already!" And not waiting for an answer, he gave Hershele a pull towards the door before the last prayer was over.

"Reb Borekh, I won't go with you against my will," Hershele said angrily, as he tore himself from Borekh's strong hand and hurried over to the head of the yeshiva, who was just coming to greet him.

"*Gut yontif*, Rebbe!" Hershele said, embracing his dear teacher.

"*Gut yontif, gut yor!*" the rebbe replied amiably. He looked Hershele over for a moment and said the traditional congratulations for new clothing. "The cut is a bit German, if you ask me, but that's not bad. 'Look not at the pitcher but at what's in it!'"

"The tailor cut it this way," Hershele answered. "I had nothing to say about it."

"It's fine. Perhaps it can be altered later. Akh, too German!"

"The style doesn't bother me at all," said Borekh. "He's a young man; this is probably the fashion these days. What do you say, Rebbe? He's so stubborn; he doesn't want to come to our house for Passover. Is that right?"

The head of the yeshiva knew that Hershele had already been invited to Brayndl's and answered pleasantly, "Reb Borekh, you say: 'He's eaten our charity meal every week for a year, so he's obligated to visit us during Passover.' And Brayndl the widow says: 'He's eaten our charity meal every week as well, so he belongs with us on Passover.' It's like this: if Hershele were an object—a garment for example, as when the question is addressed in the Gemara —I would judge, 'Let there be an equal division.' You take one half, and Brayndl can take the other. But how should the law be applied to Hershele since he's not a garment—not an object that can be divided? What then? He is a man with one body, one soul. He can't be with you and with Brayndl at the same time. The judgment must be: 'The one who gets him first wins him.' In other words, he shall go to the one who invites him first. It seems to me, you yourself admitted Brayndl invited him first."

"That's Gemara, Rebbe. I never studied Gemara!" said Borekh. "I simply think Brayndl's invitation is of a lesser significance than mine. You know, we've spoken about this."

"Who asks what you think?" the rebbe replied. "What you think is of no consequence. I have an opinion and so does Hershele. In today's world, who can give advice? I've also asked him to be with us for the holiday, and one might think a rebbe's invitation would take precedence—nevertheless, when he told me Brayndl asked him first, I understood he rightly wanted to go there, and do not begrudge it. One should choose one's path with unforced will. Nobody can compel you, Hershele. Go to Brayndl's in good health!"

"Rebbe—" Hershele began, but couldn't say another word.

"Go, eat your food with joy and drink your wine with a good heart. God is pleased with your deeds," the rebbe said and offered him his hand.

If Hershele hadn't been so shy, he would have brought the rebbe's dear hand to his lips and given it a thousand kisses. He heard and understood the reproach in his rebbe's words, but also his forgiveness and true loyalty.

"So, will you not come to my home at all during Passover? Not even once to say the blessings?" Borekh asked.

"Why not, Reb Borekh?" Hershele replied. "Since you've asked me, it will be a great honor!"

"I do ask—come in the morning for the blessings; and when you've arrived at our house, then we'll see!"

"*Gut yontif!*" said Hershele.

"*Gut yor!*" Borekh responded and called for the Slutsker to accompany him home. "All is not yet lost," he thought to himself. "I'm to blame for not asking him last week, or two weeks ago. It's true, Brayndl invited him earlier."

* * * * *

Brayndl had been waiting for her seder celebrator. When Hershele finally arrived, dressed up and excited after his talk with Borekh and the rebbe, he shone so handsomely she hardly recognized him.

"You must be wealthy already, Hershele!" she said. "You're glowing so brightly I hardly know you."

"He's already rich, Mama!" offered Mirele with a charming smile, then turning to Hershele she announced, "Come to the seder."

She led him into the next room so her mother wouldn't notice how she blushed with love at seeing him so happy and handsome. All the candles were burning and light from the big silver candelabra shone on the expensive crystal glasses, china cups, and silver-edged tableware laid out for Passover.

Brayndl showed Hershele to the place of honor at the head of the table and then took a soft chair to his right. Mirele sat across from her mother at the edge of the table. Opposite Hershele sat Deborah the serving maid, who swelled with pride at seeing her good young mistress so radiant with joy and delight.

Mirele poured the wine, and Hershele recited Kiddush with the customary and beloved tune. It seemed to Brayndl she'd heard this voice before; the passage seemed so familiar. She suddenly remembered when, as a young bride, she first heard her beloved husband chant such a Kiddush. The scene had been identical, she thought; he glowed and his voice rang out in the same manner. Oh, how happy she was back then. Now, she was a widow. How quickly the world turns.

She glanced at her daughter and wondered if she, too, had similar feelings. But Mirele was not thinking about the past. She just sang along quietly as Hershele recited the Kiddush.

As she turned to look at Hershele, a sudden thought flew through Brayndl's mind that even embarrassed her. Afraid Mirele might notice, she drove the thought away by lifting up her wine glass and taking a drink. "Very good wine," she said, "what a pleasure!"

Hershele endeared himself further as he read from the Haggadah. Brayndl had always lagged in the reading of Hebrew, while her husband, of blessed memory, had rushed through the Haggadah like a train. She'd read quietly so as not to hold up the men, and so they wouldn't notice her mistakes. She often skipped whole passages, and the little she could read aloud was always rushed. She never tasted the full flavor of the Haggadah, and so as not to feel guilty before the Master of the Universe, when she awoke the next morning, she'd always start from the beginning and recite the whole Haggadah to herself.

This evening Hershele spoke with such a sweet voice, the melody seemed to explain the words. She heard and understood everything. He didn't rush. The music, coming from his throat, was light as a bird's. His words came out clean as pearls, and she easily followed everything in the text. She had enough time to enter the station before the train took off again.

Mirele sang along with him, word for word, drawing out the melody in his manner. Yet she often arrived at the station sooner, and was happy to wait as Hershele came up behind her singing in the same timbre.

Deborah the serving maid was also pleased, and quietly recited the words of the Haggadah with them. She glanced at Mirele, then Hershele, and silently wished with her whole heart: "May you be sitting together like this next year as bride and groom. Mirele, you couldn't hope for anyone more handsome!"

"Thank you, Hershele, for not hurrying," said Brayndl. "I'm enjoying it so much, I could sit here for hours."

"You see, Mama?" Mirele said brightly. "When you listen to me, you never go wrong! To think you would have asked some old Jew to lead our seder. Oy!" Then, like a happy child, Mirele began imitating the "old Jews" of previous years as they recited the Haggadah. She mimicked them so well, Brayndl rocked with laughter.

"You shouldn't carry on like this, my daughter, laughing at old men!" Brayndl said. "You'll be old yourself one day. Your mother's already an elderly woman."

"No, Mama, I keep reminding you that you're young and pretty!" Mirele threw herself on her mother's neck with kisses and unusual tenderness.

During the meal, Brayndl showed her pleasure by giving Hershele the choicest pieces of meat and fish, and stood over him, urging him to eat more and more. With a mother's tenderness she cut his food, pleased to watch as he swallowed every bite. She gazed upon him as if she were in love with him herself, and never noticed the loving looks Mirele gave him, Hershele's shy answering smiles, or the knowing glances from the serving maid, who watched the couple with such pride.

During the second half of the seder, Brayndl's eyes began to close. The wine, the food, and the sweet voices of the children, cast a drowsy spell. She dreamed upon her soft chair, and Mirele's glance told Deborah it was time to prepare her mother's bed.

When Brayndl awoke, she made a sleepy blessing over the last cup of wine, took a sip, and said, "Next year in Jerusalem." And with her glass still raised, she blessed her good child: "Next year, with your true destined love leading the seder, and my eyes still here to see it." Brayndl then arose from the table and went to her room.

Once Brayndl had gone to bed, the real concert began. Mirele sang a song she learned from her father while sitting on his lap. Hershele answered with prayers, melodies, and playful ditties, no longer feeling like a desolate stranger. Mirele, who understood him, sang along, and together they performed a wonderful concert for the serving maid, who didn't dare to clap and shout, "Bravo!"

Finally they sang "Chad Gadya"—"Blessed be He who came and killed the Angel of Death, who killed the butcher"—and then there was nothing left to sing.

"I don't want to leave the table," Mirele said. "I'd rather talk and sing with you all night long—how could anyone sleep now?"

"Let's sing the Song of Songs!" Hershele suggested. He quickly brought in a prayer book from the other room, and, mixing Hebrew with Yiddish, began chanting the verses.

Though he knew all the Psalms were holy and the Song of Songs was the holiest of all, he never entertained the notion that the Shulammite was anything more than a symbol for the people *Yisroel.* Yet now he felt the words were made to measure for his Shulammite, Mirele. She came closer to see the words and pressed her burning cheek against his. He felt her body, her warmth, her heartbeats, and his heart pounded, too. Who could be as lovely or dear as she?

The holy words of the Song of Songs gave him courage as he recited, "Behold, you are beautiful, my beloved. Your eyes are like doves." She opened her pretty eyes and looked at him with love, and as he looked back at her he sang, "Your lips are like a scarlet thread, your words are beautiful."

As he continued to chant, he began feeling embarrassed by the words. He sang them quietly, but raised his voice when he reached the verse, "Come with me from Lebanon, my bride." As he sang the melody, he forgot who and where he was. He seemed to be there in Lebanon. "Look from the top of Mount Amana, from the peaks of Senir and Hermon, from the lions' dens, from the mountains of the leopards. You have ravished my heart, my sister, my bride!"

Mirele laid her head on his shoulder and gazed at him with such loving tenderness that his voice grew weaker. With all his strength he chanted, "You have taken my heart with one glance of your eye, with one bead of your beautiful necklace."

Mirele sang softly, "Be a brother to me, Hershele," as if she were saying, "If I came upon you in the middle of the street, I'd fall on your neck and kiss you, Hershele, and no one would scold me."

"I swear to you, Mirele, you beautiful daughter of Jerusalem," he wanted to say, "don't further awaken the love that already burns within me. Waters cannot slake it; rivers cannot put out the flame!"

Yet, before another word was spoken, the serving maid returned. She told them the clock had already struck one, and the Christian hired to extinguish the candles had just arrived.

"Good night, Hershele," Mirele whispered as she took his hand and pressed it tightly in hers.

"Good night, Mirele," he answered, barely able to utter the words.

A few minutes later, when the maid finally left her bedroom, Mirele stood by the door and whispered again, "Good night, Hershele."

Thirteen

The next morning, Hershele led the prayer service in the study house. Men grew excited, women peered through the curtained partition of the women's *shul.* Everyone asked, "Who's praying? Who can this be?"

Brayndl spoke up: "It's my Hershele!"

"What do you mean, *your* Hershele?" a woman asked.

"My yeshiva student, who eats with me, who led my seder last night," Brayndl replied.

"There's been a diamond languishing among us," said another woman. "How did we overlook him? God only opened Borekh's eyes to lift this jewel up for his child! One should ask the All-High, why such a glory has come to Borekh?"

"This is the first I've heard about it," Brayndl said. "Well, well, he's a respectable young man with rich uncles and aunts. When he's ready to return home, they'll provide for him so he won't have to listen to any proposals from Borekh."

Borekh's wife was also in the women's *shul* and proudly boasted this was *her* Hershele. She only complained about evil meddlers who had nothing better to do than get mixed up in someone else's affairs. Their time would be better spent congratulating her daughter Soreh-Feyge for the happiness the Blessed One had sent her.

Borekh also heard Hershele chanting the morning prayers, and witnessed the commotion he caused in the congregation, but it didn't make him happy. On the contrary, his heart hurt from all the praise people heaped on Hershele, as if they would tear him away, pouring salt in his wounds.

His heart told him Hershele wasn't destined for his daughter. Every day, it seemed, Hershele's stock rose—and the more Hershele's luck shone, the more his own daughter's luck faded. Borekh trembled as he thought, "Perhaps Hershele is really not for my daughter. Perhaps Brayndl is thinking to snare him for her only child. Why not? Will a fellow who chants prayers like this be left to languish? I can't win in a bidding war with Brayndl." And again, he went home without Hershele.

"What good are you, my piece of misery?" shouted Borekh's wife when her husband arrived home alone. "Go see, your daughter has no eyes left from all her crying. It's *Tishah b'Av* with her, not Passover, but do her tears worry her father?"

"What can I do if her luck is bad?" answered Borekh angrily. "Did a rich uncle have to turn up now and send him money for clothes fit for a monarch? Did God have to advise Brayndl to suddenly lift Hershele up and become his redeemer? Perhaps Hershele is just not destined for us."

Borekh's words shook his wife like thunder. "Not destined for us?" she asked in disbelief. "What are you saying? What kind of a world am I living in?"

Borekh told her the whole sad story from beginning to end, but she just couldn't comprehend it. "What do you mean, 'He doesn't want to?' What do you mean, 'Brayndl has him?'" The story fell on her like thieves robbing her beloved child in broad daylight! She couldn't allow it. She began quarreling with her husband, calling him a cold fish for not standing up for his daughter.

Borekh could no longer bear the undeserved abuse from his wife and the unrelenting tears from his daughter. In anger, he picked up a plate and threw it across the room, breaking it in pieces. An uproar ensued with his wife shrieking, "He's drunk!" and Soreh-Feyge laying a few slaps on Borekh's hand. Borekh erupted in rage, and a great fury broke loose in the house.

Nobody was at the table except the Slutsker, who ate alone, worried and afraid. As soon as he returned to the study house, he told everyone about his "joyful holiday."

The first day of Passover passed pleasurably for Hershele; he studied Chumash with Mirele and felt he understood it even better than before. Brayndl was also present for the lesson and enjoyed hearing his explanations as he read fluently from the holy Torah. He was dearer to her with every moment that passed.

"Study with her, my son," she encouraged him. "Teach her the wisdom of our holy Torah. She should know how to be a good Jewish daughter—a pious, educated Jewess. This is what her good father—may he rest in peace—always wished for her. He'll petition God for your happiness, my son, and my eyes will yet see you proud!"

Hershele and Mirele didn't simply study together. They also sang together and went out walking in the evening with Brayndl. People saw the couple together and wondered, talked, and whispered. Nothing untoward was seen, but compromising situations were imagined.

During a conversation with holiday guests, Brayndl couldn't praise Hershele enough. She innocently reported, "My Mirele nearly faints when she hears his footsteps, and always asks me, 'Mama, why didn't God give me such a lovable brother?' My lonely child, poor thing! A brother like that, blessed by God, is really a great joy!"

"Listen, Brayndl, your Mirele doesn't know how to behave with him," warned her sister-in-law. "I would absolutely never have believed her capable of such behavior if my own eyes hadn't seen it!"

"What did you see, Rebekah?" Brayndl asked fearfully.

"Sha, don't be afraid," her sister-in-law calmed her. "God forbid, I haven't seen anything disgraceful. But she's a maiden; she looks at him with such eyes! Listen, a girl's heart is like a match—it shouldn't be kindled into a hellish fire. You think he isn't handsome? You think he doesn't have fine attributes? You think she doesn't have eyes?"

"What are you talking about?" Brayndl laughed. "You think I don't know my own daughter? You think I'm wrong about him? He studies all day; you think I don't see them together? She looks upon him as a brother. She knows, poor thing, my golden child, what he's lacking, and she always complains, 'Mama, why isn't he my brother?'"

"Nevertheless, sister-in-law, I tell you, you should pay attention. He may truly be a pious boy, a kosher child. But what will you do if, God forbid, your Mirele should one day sigh over him? How will it suit you if some day people blame you for his not becoming Borekh's son-in-law? Listen, nice people's tongues—may they dry up and fall out—are already wagging."

And if these words weren't enough, Brayndl's sister-in-law also upbraided Mirele for behaving like a child. She told her what people were saying about her in the city. She reminded her she was now a young woman—may she live to be one hundred and twenty—and soon to be eighteen years old. "He's a boy, true, a fine one with many merits, but how can he compare to you? If he's too good for Borekh's crude daughter, he'll find another who's on his level. But for you, Mirele, how can he be worthy? Feh, a disgrace, my word, to have to speak to you this way!"

That same day, just before afternoon prayers, Mirele's uncle, the head of the synagogue and one of the wealthiest men of the study house, called Hershele over and glared at him coldly. "Hershele," he said sternly, "do you think you can put on a new suit of clothes and forget who you are?"

"Why would you think I've forgotten who I am?" Hershele summoned the courage to ask.

"You ask why? Because people say so. But I don't believe them. Remember, Hershele, who you are! I'm reminding you: 'There is no penalty without warning.' Understand?" And without saying another word, Mirele's uncle dropped his eyes to his Gemara as if nothing had happened.

Not long after, Hershele's friends also warned him to be careful of Borekh. "Borekh can turn the world over!" said one of the yeshiva boys. "Tonight at prayers he went to Mirele's uncle—who had me in for Passover—and gave him a piece of his mind: 'That rascal!' he shouted. 'Seemingly such a quiet lamb. He flirted with my daughter! What does she know? He promised to be her bridegroom with my permission. Now, he's gone back on his word, and it's costing me health and blood. He takes my good intentions and throws them in my face. Now he's turning your niece's head— Brayndl's only daughter—because naturally, she's more valuable merchandise. But he has the intent of a hooligan, and it hurts my heart. Really, why should I be silent?'"

"What did the head of the synagogue say?" asked another yeshiva boy while Hershele sat silently in distress.

"He just laughed and said, 'Borekh, you're drunk! Go home and sleep it off. Then get up and pat your girl on both cheeks— let's hope she's not such a fool in the future! And you can also try having a word with my sister's Mirele. I tell you, things will work out. Now go back where you came from!'

"But Borekh was even angrier and swore that first he was going to twist your head off. Then he was going to beat you; kill you! Watch out for him, Hershele!"

Now Hershele believed what Mirele's uncle had told him earlier, and a new stone was added to the weight on his heart.

When he arrived at Brayndl's that evening, Hershele found Mirele looking sad and pale, and though he saw no tears on her face, his heart suspected she'd been crying. He wanted to talk with her, but Brayndl was always nearby, and Mirele didn't begin a conversation.

Reflecting on her sister-in-law's seemingly helpful words, Brayndl reviled and cursed her angrily. "I'm not running a tavern here. Scoundrels aren't visiting my Mirele and bringing her gifts!" Nevertheless, the warnings lingered in her mind. "Let me be as fearful of my own sins as I am of my Mirele's. Just what does her easy manner with him indicate? She loves his singing. I'd swear nothing more than that has entered her head. So where's the harm? I, myself, would give a bit of my soul to hear him sing.

"And I'll vouch for him, too, that he isn't planning anything improper. Really, you can see it: he spends all his time reading. Book after book this whole Passover; he's turned over my whole bookcase. If you didn't remind him to eat and drink, he'd never leave that bookcase! Just compare him to the other boys who spend the whole Passover week gobbling, swallowing, and stuffing themselves.

"And thanks to him, Mirele's barely left the house the whole week. She studies and sings, and doesn't go sashaying down the street like all those indecent girls. Ah, my sister-in-law says: 'A girl, a boy—people talk.' Let them be struck dumb! Why should I worry? I'll pay more attention; I'll see for myself."

From that moment on, Brayndl spent the whole evening watching Hershele and Mirele, minute by minute, never leaving them alone for a moment. Hershele felt the clear sky over his head being darkened by clouds. A cold wind blew in thunderstorms that blocked the beloved sun that had made his whole world bright and beautiful.

Mirele, for her part, was beginning to take her aunt's insulting words to heart; she cried herself out before realizing it might be better to conceal her outrage. She wasn't afraid of her mother. "I can easily manage her," she said to herself, "but I'm afraid of my aunt and uncle! They won't harm me, but I worry about Hershele. He's alone. Who'll defend him should they unleash their anger on him? If only it weren't Passover, I'd tell him everything in a letter. That he must travel far away. That I'll wait my whole life for him. That I'm not worried about the future; God will show us the way!"

In lieu of a letter, she settled for merely sending him loving, consoling glances to reassure him she wasn't angry. Once she got a chance to say a few quick words to him: "Don't lose heart, Hershele, don't lose hope! As God is our witness, the more they try to tear us apart, the more I'll stand by you. Don't worry, someday we'll look back on all this suffering and laugh. Tomorrow, I'll explain everything in a letter. Remember, God is our witness!"

Before Mirele could say another word, Brayndl returned with an air of suspicion, although she remained silent. To calm her mother's mistrust, Mirele offered to go along to her uncle's house to finish Passover.

Hershele remembered he hadn't visited his good rebbe during the holiday, though he'd been graciously invited and had promised to come. During the first days of Passover, he'd told Mirele about his rebbe's kindness and loyalty. Though he'd said nothing specific, Mirele knew how much the head of the yeshiva meant to him—and perhaps his daughter as well.

"While you're out, I'll go visit my rebbe," Hershele said, preparing to leave.

With a tinge of jealousy, Mirele quickly said, "No, you must stay here until we get back!"

"Yes, stay here," Brayndl agreed. "You're never sad when you have a book to study. And meanwhile, the maid hasn't come back yet, and it's never good to leave the house unattended. Please stay, I beg of you!"

Hershele remained, alone amidst all the beautifully appointed rooms. Everything here had become so beloved and dear to him. The table where he'd first seen Mirele; where she'd first said a friendly word to him. And there, by the mirror, they stood together, hand in hand. He'd said her name and seen her pale face redden. He felt again, as he had then, an agreeable trembling in his whole body. He looked at himself in the mirror, pale as he was then, perhaps even paler, but now alone, all alone. Mirele was at her uncle's, and God knows what was being said to her. He turned away. His eyes flew over the room as if seeking a way to protect her from her uncle's words.

He walked to the window and saw the sun sinking behind a mountain of dark clouds. It seemed to bend and bow to him, as if giving a final farewell from afar. His heart grew sad and heavy; he paced back and forth across the room. "Is there a palace in the world which could be as beloved and dear to me as this house, this room? The sun is setting as it always does; it doesn't care that a wonderful sun has set for me, a radiant and beloved sun."

Where the sun had risen that morning, dark night was now intruding, draping the town so sadly, so coldly. "Oh, you dark, cold night!" Hershele thought. "For whom are you as terrible as you are for me? Perhaps even now the multitude of angels are crying, 'Sinning souls, the wicked shall return to hell!' Although I haven't sinned, why am I hearing the voices cry, 'Back, back! The holiday is over; Paradise is gone, go back!' Where shall I go now? Return to the poor yeshiva from this radiant, beloved house?

"No, I can't go back there again. Who is hurt by my being here? What do you want, uncles and aunts? Leave us in peace; don't hinder us. Don't be the serpent in our Garden of Eden! Oh, people are so cruel. And God? Never before has Your way seemed so hard to understand. Do you want me to have neither Paradise nor the woman who offered me the Tree of Knowledge? Good. I'll leave. I'll leave here, but give me Mirele! Give me advice, knowledge, and wisdom, so I can find Paradise for us. Give me strength to endure my longing and pain. I don't ask for more; I don't need more."

While Hershele was speaking the thoughts of his heavy heart to the four empty walls, Mirele's aunt was accosting her niece with tales of woe that can befall an unsuspecting girl from a too-friendly word or an excessive glance, God forbid. Mirele heard it all and remained silent, though she felt her blood boiling in her veins.

Today, contrary to his usual custom, her uncle mixed into the women's conversation, belittling Hershele in every way possible. "He's a nobody, a nothing! Is Borekh the butcher's family not good enough for him? He's such a fine person? What a joke! Borekh will show him a thing or two. Feh on such a hooligan!"

No longer able to control herself, Mirele blurted out: "Why are you so angry, Uncle? Hershele hasn't done anything to you."

Her uncle didn't answer; he took the tip of his beard into his mouth, biting the hairs mercilessly, looking at Mirele as if he wanted to say, 'Lucky you're a guest in my house; otherwise, I'd slap your cheeks for being so disrespectful." Mirele felt his gaze, but didn't reveal her anger. Her heart grew more constricted by the minute.

"Listen," he said to Brayndl when Mirele was with her cousins in another room, "It's you who deserve judgment, not she! She's a child with a child's sense, but you should be smarter than that. Her silence tells me more than her words. I'm afraid she's gone too far with him!"

Brayndl tried to defend herself and her daughter, and Hershele as well. But the uncle wouldn't listen. "I'll box his ears when I find him!" he shouted. "I'm going to make Havdalah—the difference between Shabbes and the week—and afterwards, I'll show Hershele the difference between Borekh and me!"

Brayndl's hands and feet trembled upon hearing this. She knew her brother's anger and feared he could kill him! She knew Hershele wasn't to blame for Borekh's drunken accusations, and what could be expected from Mirele, poor thing? "No, I mustn't leave things this way," she told herself. "Not a hair on his head should be hurt. Men become such wild animals when the frenzy strikes them!"

So as not to cause a scandal, Brayndl left quietly and hurried home. The minute she came through the door, she begged Hershele, "Go, son, leave quickly! Why does such trouble befall me, Master of the Universe? So much misery to come from my good deeds! Hershele, have I sinned by welcoming you into our family? And how is my good child to blame, poor thing, that people should bathe in her blood?"

"What's happened?" Hershele asked fearfully.

"Borekh has defamed you to my brother with lies and slander. It's best you leave now. He might come and beat you. That man's a wild beast!"

"He might beat me?" Hershele gasped, blood flooding into his pale cheeks.

"Only if he sees you, my son," Brayndl consoled him. "Don't let him find you while he's angry. You'll see, once he's cooled off, everything will be as before. May I have such good defenders in the next world as you have in this world with me and my good Mirele. Don't we know you? Do you think we believe what that drunkard Borekh says?"

"Thank you for your kindness, Brayndl," said Hershele in a broken voice. "I'll obey and leave now, though the indignity of fleeing devastates me. I beg you, don't think ill of me, and I hope your brother will love me again some day."

"Let God himself have such good thoughts of me as I have of you," Brayndl said. "Tomorrow, my son, I'll send for you. Don't be downhearted. You are, God forbid, not alone. Go quickly. I'm trembling lest he come."

Hershele looked at the house as if for the last time, as if bidding farewell to everything that had become so dear and beloved to him. "Say goodbye to your kind Mirele for me," he said in a trembling voice. "Tell her neither she nor I is guilty of anything. People who can't allow others happiness are the ones at fault!"

Brayndl saw tears in his eyes as he opened the door and headed out into the street. Fifteen minutes later, Mirele came home with her aunt and cousins. "Where is your uncle?" Brayndl asked uneasily.

"My husband stopped to talk with the new bailiff," said Brayndl's sister-in-law.

"I expect he'll invite the bailiff here," Brayndl said. "Goodness, daughter, how embarrassing; I don't have any liquor to welcome him with. He's often said he'd come by to eat fish at my table. I don't require his services, but it's always best to stay in the good graces of such people."

A while later, the uncle arrived without the bailiff. He soon recited the evening prayers, made Havdalah, and when he was finished, acted kind and tender to his sister and the other guests. He even apologized to Mirele for his earlier rantings. "What's true is true," he said. "Hershele does have merits. He's no scoundrel. But I'm really angry with today's children. In our day, we would've never thought of dressing up and getting entangled with maidens. You think I'm suspicious of him? That he turned the head of Borekh's daughter the way Borekh screams? God forbid! I don't think it went that far, but he did have contact with her, and that's not proper. Otherwise, it's not my concern!"

Though she tried to control herself, Mirele's uncle's softer words caused big teardrops to roll down her burning cheeks. "Why are you crying, my child?" Brayndl asked, attempting to calm her. Her uncle also tried to comfort her, but his efforts only made matters worse. The women sprinkled her with water and tried to cool her with strong vinegar, but Mirele cried quietly, unable to answer.

Hershele wandered the darkened streets in confusion, angry at himself for deserting Mirele. "I should have stayed," he told himself, then reconsidered. "Perhaps it's better this way."

Another thought came into his mind: "What if Mirele's unable to endure the disgrace? What if she changes her mind? No, no! She swore, 'God is our witness!'"

He implored God to give him strength to withstand temptation—all temptations. He grew a bit calmer and walked on until he reached the bridge. The water was high; the river rushed past with enormous strength. Confused thoughts flew through his head. "Where's the water going? What drives it? What's pushing it onward? Why does it seethe so? And what of mankind? What are we in comparison to the power that drives the mighty river?"

A terrible thought came into his head: to throw himself into the rushing waters. To swim or be dragged far away; to become one with the unyielding elements that never rest, that go their way without ever asking anyone's permission.

"How good it is when there's no alternative," he said to himself. "But I am a human being with free will. I must make my own way! Yet, how may I choose if others impede me?" His head began to spin; he thought he heard a voice coming from the river, "See how we're driven! Come, jump in and that will be the end!" A powerful force drew him towards the water. "Wouldn't it be easier for everyone," he told himself, "if I ended it all now?"

He raised his eyes and suddenly a figure came into view. Was this Mirele, in a long white dress? The figure's sad head was bowed; wind blew her lovely curls from side to side. She walked, wringing her hands, moving slowly along the riverbank in search of something. "What are you seeking; whom are you seeking? Don't search, Mirele, I'm here, I'm alive!" he called out to her as he ran from the bridge, but the figure had vanished. "It was only an apparition," he tried to convince himself.

Uncertain where he was going, Hershele wandered away from the terrible river, and soon found himself standing in front of Brayndl's house. All the shutters were closed and he could see no visible lights inside. The street was very quiet; he seemed to hear the sound of crying coming from a window. He stretched out his hand to knock on the door. Perhaps he could ask the maid how

Mirele was doing, but he lacked the courage and dropped his out-stretched hand.

"Last night I, too, rested under this beloved roof," his heart reminded him. Tears choked him and his heart constricted; he rested on the porch to keep from fainting. Rain began to fall, and though he felt the drops, he tried to ignore them. But as the rain increased minute by minute, Hershele reluctantly headed to the study house.

The door was open as usual. Wet and fully awakened by the rain, Hershele entered quietly and looked around. Everyone was sound asleep and had been for several hours. Hershele felt exhausted and weak; his hands and feet were shaking. He tried to sit and rest on a bench in the corner, but his heart pounded and his mind raced. A thousand thoughts came to him. He remembered the sad story of the Vilner Balebesl. He imagined him sitting here in the study house, his head bent down and sadness in his handsome face. Hershele asked himself, "Who knows what's in my heart? Who knows how much I suffer?" and he heard the Balebesl's voice in response, "I know; I feel your heartache!"

"Such terrible suffering," Hershele's trembling lips stammered, and he quietly began to sing the Balebesl's song from the book of penitential prayers. His voice grew deeper, stronger, and more moving, until it awoke all the yeshiva boys, who ran to him barefoot and afraid.

"What's happened to you, Hershele?" the Vilner asked in fear. "You're soaking wet!"

Hershele didn't answer; he just kept singing. Suddenly his voice broke, and he fell on the Vilner's neck. He pressed his face to his friend's shoulder and cried brokenheartedly. Confused, the Vilner tried to calm him by taking hold of his cold trembling hands. "Fetch water, a bit of cold water!" the Vilner called to the others. "Donkeys, why are you just standing there?"

Several boys ran to the washstand, but it was dry. They looked everywhere, but there wasn't a drop of water in the whole study house.

"Borekh the butcher, may his name be blotted out," said one of the boys quietly. "Borekh's caught and beat Hershele, let him be struck by lightning!"

Finally, the Vilner succeeded in getting Hershele to sit down. "Tell me everything that's in your heart," he soothed him.

"Nothing, nothing," answered Hershele, sobbing. "Oh, how I wish I could die!"

Suddenly heavy steps were heard in the study house. Before they could look up, a Russian officer was standing before them with the bailiff and a few policemen.

"Who are you? What are you doing here?" he asked with a loud wild voice burning with wrath. Some of the boys quietly snuck out; the rest looked at him in terror.

"What do you mean, who are we? What are we doing here?"

"Do you have passports?" the Russian officer asked gruffly.

Everyone was silent. Only the chattering of teeth could be heard.

"Take them away!" the Russian officer commanded the policemen.

In the ensuing scuffle, a few of the boys jumped out the window and escaped. The rest let themselves be dragged away like prisoners.

"'I am with you in your troubles,'" the Vilner reminded Hershele as he held tightly to his hand. "Borekh is doing this to us to get back at you."

Hershele pressed closer to his friend in fear of being separated from him, but when they arrived at the police station, he was pulled away to a different room. The Vilner was led to a cell with all the other boys.

*   *   *   *   *

The next morning during the prayer service, the study house boiled. Not one of the cantor's words was heard. In vain, Mirele's uncle, the head of the synagogue, banged on his prayer stand for quiet, but the crowd wouldn't stop talking.

"Such villainy! What a thing to do! This trouble is all Borekh's doing, may his name be blotted out! He doesn't even care about this defamation."

The head of the yeshiva wrung his hands and complained to Mirele's uncle: "Why are you silent? Why aren't you doing something for the boys? Remember the mitzvah of redeeming prisoners. This is a disgrace for the whole town. This is how, God forbid, the whole yeshiva could be destroyed!"

A few older householders also spoke to the head of the synagogue: "You're our most influential community leader; how could you allow something so vile to happen?"

Calmly and coldly Mirele's uncle continued praying, word after word, until he had completed the *Aleinu*. "Don't shout," he said as he peacefully put away his prayer shawl. "Nobody is eating them there. 'There is justice and law in the land.' I'll go find out. The Russian officer himself will tell me what he wants and who betrayed Hershele. I think I can get them released."

Relieved, the crowd calmed down; people knew the head of the synagogue was the Russian officer's right-hand man. Half the town accompanied him to the police station, but only he was granted entry. Meanwhile, as the townsfolk remained in the street awaiting the outcome, people began expressing their opinions.

They cursed Borekh and accused him of taking his revenge on Hershele for breaking the engagement.

In the middle of the chatter, Borekh arrived, surprised and frightened. He'd heard the whole story in the street and ran to save Hershele.

An old Jew fell on him angrily: "You enemy of *Yisroel!* You coarse villain! You should be gutted like a fish!"

Not understanding, Borekh asked innocently, "What do you want from me? How is this my fault?"

"You should be sentenced to a donkey's burial for giving our Jews over to the *goyim.*"

Borekh swore he had nothing to do with it, and no matter what the price, he'd do whatever it took to free Hershele. Yet no one believed him, and they tried to prove by various arguments why this crisis was all his doing. Angrily, Borekh cursed them and began bargaining with the policemen at the door to let him in.

A few of the policemen tried to drive away the crowd, but their efforts were futile. When two were pushed aside, ten others appeared in their places. The circle grew even greater and louder.

Finally, Mirele's uncle came out and quieted the crowd. "It was hard, even for me," he called out, "but I've succeeded completely!" A short time later the yeshiva students were released. As they hurried from the police station, they were bombarded with a thousand questions.

Only the head of the yeshiva noticed that Hershele was not among them. "Where's Hershele?" he asked Mirele's uncle with concern.

"Am I Hershele's keeper?" Mirele's uncle answered tersely.

"What do you mean? You just said they were all released!"

"Don't trouble yourself over him; he's fine. He had the good sense to pay a bribe, and since he wasn't arrested under the same charges as the others, the police have arranged for his immediate release."

"And if he isn't released?"

"If I say he'll be released, believe it! Listen, children," Mirele's uncle said turning to the yeshiva students. "First of all, don't be hooligans. Understand what I mean? Second: within a month you should receive passports granting you permission to remain here. Third: those who don't receive passports should leave the area. This time I've prevailed, but the next time, who knows? Remember, 'It's not possible to get away without a price.'"

Though many in the crowd didn't understand the meaning of the head of the synagogue's words, many praised him for his efforts. "What would've happened if our community leader were like all those other rich men who don't care what happens to us?" they asked each other.

Meanwhile, Borekh made his way into the police station where he found Hershele still being held. Mirele's uncle hadn't pleaded for him, and since he had no passport to remain in town, the police planned to send him back home with the military convoy. Borekh begged them to reconsider, and promised whatever was necessary to have Hershele released, but it was of no use.

When the clock struck three, Borekh suddenly remembered Hershele hadn't had anything to eat since being imprisoned. Like an arrow shot from a bow, he flew home to grab a pot of food. He then ran back, buying from street vendors a small loaf of white bread, tea with sugar, a pair of oranges, and a piece of veal that had been promised to the synagogue secretary. Arriving at the police station, he was let in to see the prisoner.

Tears welled up in Borekh's eyes when he saw the dead-white Hershele sitting in the dark and dirty little cell. "Hershele!" he exclaimed, as the food pot nearly dropped from his hand. "Don't worry, it may cost me half my life, but I'll get you out of here."

Hershele looked up at him sadly.

"I have such dark luck," Borekh said in a pained voice. "For my good deeds this is how I'm thanked! You, too, probably believe I'm at fault. Listen, Hershele, let my bones rot in prison and let me never be released if I knew anything about this before now. The truth will rise like oil on water. Let me just get you out of here; you yourself will see. Meanwhile, poor thing, you're bewildered and frightened. It's upsetting to see you this way. Eat something."

But Hershele made no move towards the food.

"It wasn't Brayndl, your redeemer, who remembered to bring you food, but I, Borekh, your supposed enemy."

Hershele looked at Borekh again, and Borekh saw big teardrops in his eyes. It seemed Hershele wanted to say something, but his lips were tightly drawn together, and he hid his face in his hands. Borekh drew out his moneybag and placed a handful of change near Hershele.

"Take it, don't be left without a few coins in your pocket. I beg you, eat something. I myself haven't had a drop of cold water today. Nevertheless, I'm not going home until I get you released. Then I'll eat. Be a man, dive into this feast. Food gives us strength to withstand our troubles. Eat up, child, what are you afraid of? At least you haven't been arrested as a thief. Courage, Hershele! I'll be back soon." Leaving the little cell, Borekh ran to the Russian officer's home, where he hoped to speak with him more freely.

The head of the yeshiva had believed Mirele's uncle when he said Hershele would be freed before all the other boys. Yet he worried that Hershele might be hiding somewhere, afraid to come back to the yeshiva. Together with the Vilner, the rebbe sought Hershele in all the synagogues, study houses, and school buildings where a yeshiva student might think to hide. As hard as they looked, they couldn't find him anywhere.

"Listen, Rebbe," the Vilner said, "my heart tells me Hershele is still in jail. So I ask, 'Why would the head of the synagogue tell a lie?' Perhaps he wanted to teach Hershele a lesson? I'm afraid to say, the whole business stems from the head of the synagogue, the supposed redeemer, himself."

"What are you saying?" the rebbe grabbed him as if bitten by a snake. "He's a very powerful man! This is a harsh accusation; I couldn't believe this even of Borekh!"

"I may be wrong, Rebbe, but let's go to Brayndl's house. Perhaps they'll know something there." Reluctantly, the rebbe agreed.

But Brayndl hadn't been out in the street yet and knew nothing. "*Gevalt!* What kind of an arrest?" she shouted, not listening to the end of the story. "This must be Borekh's work! What does my brother the head of the synagogue say?"

"First God, blessed be He; next your brother, our synagogue official," the head of the yeshiva answered. "He's gotten them all freed already."

"Let him be praised! You gave me quite a start. I haven't been able to leave the house today: my Mirele, let her be healthy, burned half the night like a fire—no evil eye, God forbid—with a fever. She's very sick, poor thing. That's all she needs, to find out Hershele's been arrested. If you just knew, Rebbe, the charm she sees in him. I myself would run to the police station to get him out if I could leave my sick child. But thank God he's been freed. Where is he now?"

"He's probably hiding somewhere; he surely hasn't eaten. We've been looking for him since noon," said the rebbe.

"Fool, what is he worried about?" Brayndl laughed. "If you find him, send him here, please—he shouldn't be afraid. Last night we thought my brother was angry at Hershele. Later, though, my brother spoke very kindly of him. But I, foolish woman that I am, worried he'd run out of here and beat Hershele. Rebbe, tell Hershele he should return. My sick Mirele's already asked for him several times, asking if he's coming to eat with us today. I wish her medicine were as well prepared as the meal we have waiting for him in the kitchen since early this morning. I love him like my own child!"

"I can't understand it," the rebbe said to the Vilner as they left Brayndl's. "How shall we, then, examine this passage? We clearly have some sort of story here. Question: Why should the head of the synagogue be so angry at Hershele? Question: Why does Brayndl say so innocently that Hershele is very charming in her eyes? And if there is no story, there's another question: What is the meaning of: 'She thought her brother was angry. Perhaps he was going to beat Hershele?' Hah! The answer: this is a larger question requiring more investigation. Vilner, let's go to the police station to see if perhaps Hershele is still imprisoned there."

Though the head of the yeshiva didn't know a word of Russian, he was certain he'd find someone at the station who would explain to the Russian officer why he was there. So off he went like a martyr, taking off his hat as he entered the police station. The Vilner, afraid of returning to the place of his previous confinement, decided to wait outside near the gate.

To his surprise, the rebbe found Borekh standing inside the police station. "What have you heard?" asked the rebbe.

"What's to hear?" Borekh answered, his lips trembling in exasperation. "Might as well be speaking to the wall! They won't listen and won't even consider letting him go."

"About letting him go? Is that the story, he's still here?"

"What do you think? He's well buried." Borekh sighed.

"As people are wont to say: 'If a fool throws a stone in the water, ten wise men cannot get it out!'" said the rebbe.

"Rebbe, perhaps you think I'm to blame for this? On the contrary! Listen to what the accusing officer says, and you'll know who cooked this up."

"What will I hear? This shames the Jewish name. Enough disgrace and indignity! Take me to see Hershele; he'll at least know people are trying to free him."

"I can't take you; I'm waiting for the man in charge," Borekh answered. "Go over there. The prison guard will let you in."

But the rebbe was afraid to go alone. "All right, come on," said Borekh as he took the rebbe's arm and showed him the way. He then hurried back to wait for the prison commander.

The guard let the rebbe go up to the cell, but wouldn't let him in. "Hershele!" called the rebbe, seeing the prisoner, his dear student, looking so forlorn.

"Rebbe!" Hershele answered, running up to the little barred window when he heard his voice. They each had tears in their eyes. They were so surprised neither could say a word.

"'Woe to me that I should see you like this,'" the rebbe sighed, quoting from the Gemara. Hershele was quiet at first, but suddenly his eyes flashed with the same fire the rebbe always saw when he had asked the boy a difficult talmudic question.

"'Happy am I to see you like this,'" Hershele said, standing up a little straighter, and in that moment, the rebbe's student seemed to grow two heads taller.

"What do you mean by that?" asked the rebbe. "Are you then Rabbi Akiva, who died a martyr's death?"

"No, rebbe, I'm not Rabbi Akiva; I'm Joseph!" he answered forcefully. "Remember the play I acted in at Purim, 'The Selling of

Joseph'? Since then my luck has played the same tricks on me as Joseph's. Like Joseph, I found charm in peoples' eyes without doing anything to deserve it. Like Joseph, I'm now a prisoner through false accusations. You'll see, Rebbe, like Joseph, I will yet become an important man, and will pay back with goodness all the evil that's befallen me."

"Truly, I wish that for you," the rebbe said, heartened by Hershele's spirit. "If they'll only release you, that will be your reward. You should go to Volozhin. If you study there, you'll become a respectable man."

"Make no mistake, Rebbe, and tell Borekh, too, I won't go to Volozhin. I'll leave the country, and I won't just study Gemara, which has caused me to be dependent on the opinions of others. Until now have I been a man? Have I had any influence over my own life? Others have given me food, a bench to sleep on, and told me what to do. If someone wants to throw me in a dark prison cell, he can do it.

"Where are my alternatives? The books of philosophy say every man is entitled to his choices. What kind of man am I that I can't even protect that which is most dear to me in life? I can't marry; and I can't do anything about it. No, I won't be such an unhappy creature from this day forward. I must become a strong and up-right man! Only wisdom and knowledge make a man. From now on, I must seek wisdom and influence. Now, Rebbe, if you under-stand me, you can make sense of my punishment. 'God is with me, and I will not fear.'"

A few minutes passed before the rebbe could reply. At first he thought Hershele's mind had been altered. Perhaps he didn't know what he was saying. Yet little by little he realized that Hershele spoke in earnest and that his thoughts weren't coming from a lunatic.

"Woe to the ears that hear this," the rebbe finally sighed. "It would be surprising if your mind wasn't affected. The entire holiday, people say, you always had a book in your hand, and it wasn't the Gemara. My heart also told me the fashionable clothes you put on would bring you to no good. An Evil Inclination is standing over you, my dear student. See how weak you are, that you can't even resist this small temptation, and are willing to become a heretic by denying the God of *Yisroel*. Return to righteousness, Hershele. Don't let the Evil Inclination prevail!" The rebbe wanted to convince Hershele that his arguments had no substance, but the jailer interrupted them and drove the old Jew from the door. "Enough chattering for five kopecks," he said. "Get lost!"

Whether the jailor was delivering his own message or a message from the Satanic Majesty, the rebbe couldn't swear. But it was clear as the sun that this was a story of Satan: that Hershele was not able to hear out the rebbe's chastisements and would not repent of his words.

As he was leaving the police station, the rebbe said to Borekh, "I don't know who imprisoned him, but I do know a dear soul has been sacrificed on the altar of impurity; sacrificed to the evil that wraps itself around everything, may heaven preserve us."

Borekh didn't understand and told the rebbe that he'd prevailed: Hershele would only be held for a few more days. Perhaps, in the meantime, a passport could be obtained for him. Both went home, one a bit consoled, the other without any comfort or hope, just as one leaves a funeral procession.

* * * * *

Early one morning as a few young shop girls were opening their stores—shop girls who still remembered the play in which the wild Midianites sent the handsome, shackled Joseph away into

Egypt to be sold as a slave—they were startled to see several prisoners being marched out of the police station. One prisoner, a
young man dressed in beautiful new clothes, looked like that very
Joseph.

Later, as the prisoners were driven down the road bound in
chains, some of those maidens who had run to get a better look,
confirmed with tears in their eyes that this was, indeed, the boy.
"His face was pale and dead," they reported, "and his head was
turned back towards Brayndl's house."

Whether he hoped Brayndl would come save him, or whether
he was silently saying goodbye to the one who was so dear to him,
they didn't know. But seeing the big teardrops in his beautiful eyes,
their hearts gave out from pity. And God alone was witness to
his loneliness.

ACKNOWLEDGEMENTS

Sincerest thanks to Jane Peppler for her English translation, and to Shalom Goldman and Sheva Zucker for their assistance with the manuscript. Thanks also to Kathleen Southern for her editing help, Arthur Clark, Lynn Padgett, and Maxine Carr for their proof-reading efforts, and Curt Leviant for his always-wise advice on the difficulties of Yiddish in translation.

I must also express my deepest gratitude to Carolyn Toben and Robin and Jim Evans for their ongoing encouragement and loving support.

Scott Hilton Davis
August 2016

GLOSSARY

Adar. The twelfth month of the Jewish year, occurring in February and March. Purim is celebrated in the month of Adar.

Aleinu. The closing prayer of all three daily prayer services.

Balebesl. A newly wed man.

bar mitzvah. The confirmation ceremony for Jewish boys when they turn thirteen.

beshert. A person's predestined soul mate. A woman's soul mate is called a *besherter;* a man's is called a *besherteh.*

bimah. The raised platform in the synagogue or prayer house on which the Torah scroll is placed for public reading and where the service leader often stands.

Borekh. Man's name that means "blessed."

bris. The ceremony of circumcision performed on a Jewish boy when he is eight days old.

chametz. Leavening which is forbidden in foods during Passover.

challah. A braided bread eaten on the Sabbath and holidays.

charoset. A sweet dish made of fruit, nuts, and spices eaten during Passover.

Chanukah. The Festival of Lights; a holiday celebrating the liberation of the Temple in Jerusalem by Judah Maccabee and his followers in the second century B.C.E.

cheder. Traditional religious elementary school.

Chumash. A book containing the five books of the Torah.

Eretz Yisroel. The land of Israel.

fräulein. German word for "Miss" or an unmarried woman.

Gehennah. Hell.

Gemara. The portion of the Talmud containing rabbinical analysis and commentary on the collection of oral laws called the Mishnah.

Gevalt. An exclamation of surprise, shock, or fear.

goyim. Gentiles; non-Jews.

gut yontif. Good holiday.

gut yontif, gut yor. Good holiday, good year.

Haggadah. A book or booklet containing the home seder service used during Passover.

Haskalah. The Jewish Enlightenment movement in the 19th century.

Havdalah. The ceremony that ends the Sabbath and holidays.

Kaddish. The mourner's prayer for the dead.

kasha. Toasted buckwheat groats.

Kiddush. The blessing over wine.

kishke. Stuffed beef intestines filled with a mixture of flour, chicken fat, onion, and seasonings.

kopeck. A small Russian coin; one one-hundredth of a ruble.

Korach. The biblical figure who challenged Moses and Aaron's authority and was buried alive by God for his rebellion. Many stories are told of Korach's wealth.

kvass. A fermented drink made from rye bread.

Love of Zion. Abraham Mapu's novel published in 1853 and thought to be the first secular novel written in biblical Hebrew. A redemptive retelling of the story of Amnon and Tamar found in 2 Samuel, the book had a profound influence on Eastern European Jewish youth during the time of the Jewish Enlightenment.

maskil. A follower or supporter of the *Haskalah.*

Megillah. The scroll containing the Book of Esther, which relates the story of Purim; a long, convoluted story.

melamud. A teacher of young children.

mitzvah. A commandment or good deed.

Montefiore. Sir Moses Montefiore (1784-1885). Born in England, he became a wealthy Jewish merchant, stockbroker, and philanthropist.

Nissan. The first month of the Jewish calendar which falls in March and April. Passover is celebrated during the month of Nissan.

Pesach. Passover.

Pirkei Avot. Ethics of the Fathers; a portion of the Mishnah, the "Oral Torah," that discusses ethics and morals.

Purim. The Feast of Lots. A joyful holiday celebrating the events in the Book of Esther that describe the victory over Haman and his oppression of Persian Jews.

Purimshpieler. An actor in a Purim play.

rabbi. A Jewish scholar, teacher, or religious leader.

rebbe. Teacher; may also be the title of a Chassidic rabbi.

rebbetzin. The rabbi's wife.

Rothschild. A wealthy family of European bankers, merchants, financiers, and philanthropists. Baron Edmond de Rothschild devoted himself to art, culture, and funding Jewish settlements in Israel.

schlimazel. A person with perpetually bad luck.

schlemiel. A foolish person.

seder. The home Passover service and supper that recounts how God liberated the Jews from Egyptian slavery.

Shabbes. The Sabbath.

Shekhinah. The earthly presence or manifestation of the Divine. In Kabbalah, the feminine attributes of the presence of the Divine.

shikse. A non-Jewish girl or woman.

shmone esrey. The eighteen blessings recited in the daily prayers.

shochet. A ritual slaughterer; a person certified to slaughter animals and poultry according to Jewish law.

shtetl. A small Jewish town or village in Russia and Eastern Europe.

shul. A synagogue or house of prayer.

Shulammite. The central female figure in the Song of Songs.

tefillin. Phylacteries; the leather boxes containing scriptures, which a Jewish man binds to his arm and forehead with leather straps during morning prayers.

Tishah b'Av. A fast day on the ninth day of Av to commemorate the destruction of the first and second Temples in Jerusalem.

tsimes. A sweet stew often made with carrots, prunes, potatoes, and other vegetables.

yeshiva. Jewish institute of higher education and talmudic learning.

yetzer hore. The Evil Inclination.

yetzer tov. The Good Inclination.

Yisroel. Israel.

Yom Kippur. The Day of Atonement.

vey iz mir. Woe is me.

Zohar. A 13th century work of Jewish mysticism that is central to the study of Kabbalah.

MEMORIES AND SCENES
SHTETL, CHILDHOOD, WRITERS

This collection of eleven autobiographical short stories by the beloved Yiddish writer Jacob Dinezon includes poignant and humorous experiences from his childhood in the shtetl, colorful characters that influenced his life, and the events that ignited his passion for writing.

A treasure trove of Jewish history, culture, and values available for the first time in English.

Translated from the Yiddish by Tina Lunson.

(ISBN 978-0-9798156-1-4)

YOSELE
A STORY FROM JEWISH LIFE

Jacob Dinezon's powerful novel describes the poverty-stricken life of a young schoolboy and exposes the outmoded and cruel teaching methods prevalent in the traditional *cheders* (Jewish elementary schools) of the late 1800s.

The outrage resulting from the book's publication produced an urgent call for reform that set the stage for the establishment of a secular schools movement in Eastern Europe.

This first-time English translation presents a rare and vivid picture of Jewish life in Eastern Europe at the turn of the 20th century.

Translated from the Yiddish by Jane Peppler.

(ISBN 978-0-9798156-3-8)